Sweet DREAMS

LADIES OF STANFORD

T. REECE

Contents

Glossary

♥

Here's the definition of Russian Terms used in this story

1. Privet - Hello

2. Moye solnyshko - My sunshine (a term of endearment)

3. Da - Yes

4. Net - No

5. Babushka - Grandmother

6. Kvass - A traditional Slavic fermented beverage made from rye bread

7. Draniki - Potato pancakes

8. Machanka - A pork stew

9. Bozhe moy - My God

10. Dosvidaniya - Goodbye

11. Dobroye utro - Good morning

12. Rhapsody (Рапсодия) - The name of Yuri's former nightclub, meaning "Rhapsody" in English

This glossary should help everyone understand the Russian terms used throughout the story

About the author

♥

As a child, Best-selling author, T. Reece also known as Ty Langston, "loved to read about dragons and knights so much that one day, her grandmother told her to "just write about them."

So she did.

From that day forward, she never left home without her pen, a notebook, and some kind of music playing in the background. Her love of reading expanded from fantasy into science fiction, and eventually into Contemporary Romance.

You can find her website at tylangston.com

or join your Facebook group at The Pied Pipers!

Subscribe to her newsletter at this link

Also by

♥

As Ty Langston
The Bet
Love In The Cirque Mistique
As Piper Reece
Coming Home
As T. Reece
Nova Springs Series
Ignite
An Unexpected Match
Second Chances
Love On Tap
The Nova Springs Box Set Books 1-4
Ladies of Stanford
Sweet Dreams

One

♥

A s Beth struggled to find the right key, her red curls absorbed the sweet aroma of cinnamon and nutmeg. A smile lingered on her lips as she pushed through the flurry of snowflakes illuminated by the porch light. Finally, she unlocked the door and stepped inside. The only sound in the house was the gentle ticking of an old grandfather clock in the hallway.

"Keith?" She called out for her longtime boyfriend as she took off her coat and hung it up. There was no response. She checked her watch, noting that it was already 6:30 p.m. He should have been home by now.

Beth made her way to the kitchen, her footsteps echoing in the silence. A half-empty wine glass sat on the counter, lipstick staining its rim. Her frown deepened. Keith didn't wear lipstick.

A thump from upstairs made her jump. Then, a muffled giggle.

Beth's heart was racing as she climbed the stairs. Her mind was a chaotic mess, conjuring up worst-case scenarios with each step. The bedroom door was slightly open, casting a thin beam of light into the dim hallway.

Another burst of laughter echoed through the room, a deep masculine rumble. It was Keith's laugh, a sound Beth knew all too well.

Her hand wavered on the doorknob before she pushed it open, her heart pounding in her chest. The scene that unfolded before her froze her blood in its veins.

Despite being in a committed relationship for three years, Keith was in bed with a blonde-haired woman. His hands gripped tightly onto the woman's hips as he moved rhythmically behind her. Her back arched and head tossed back in ecstasy; she was on all fours, crying out his name in a voice filled with raw pleasure.

Beth recognized the blonde instantly: Gina, the new fresh-faced cashier from Sweet Dreams. Keith grunted and groaned with each thrust into Gina, his muscles straining under the dim light of their bedroom. His eyes were closed tight, lost in his own world of carnal delight.

The sight of them together - Keith and Gina lost in each other - chilled Beth to her core. The sounds of their shared pleasure echoed hauntingly around the room as Beth stood frozen at the doorway, an unwilling witness to their intimate betrayal.

For a moment, the world stopped. Beth stood frozen, unable to breathe, unable to think. Then, as if someone had pressed play, everything rushed back into motion.

"Beth!" Keith scrambled to cover himself, his face a mask of shock and guilt. "I... I thought you were working late."

Gina squeaked, pulling the sheets up to her chin, her wide eyes darting between Beth and Keith.

Beth opened her mouth, but no words came out. Her chest felt tight, her vision blurry at the edges.

"Honey, I can explain," Keith started, reaching for her.

The pet name snapped Beth out of her trance. "Don't you dare 'honey' me," she hissed, her voice low and dangerous. "How long?"

Keith's mouth opened and closed like a fish out of water. "It... it's not what you think."

"How. Long?" Beth repeated each word sharply.

Gina whimpered, clutching the sheets tighter. "I'm so sorry, Beth. It just happened..."

"Just happened?" Beth's laugh was hollow. "What, you tripped and fell on his dick?"

Keith winced. "Beth, please. Let's talk about this."

"Talk?" Beth's voice rose, hysteria creeping in. "You want to talk now? After I catch you in OUR bed with one of MY employees?"

She turned to Gina, who shrank back against the headboard. "And you. I gave you a job when no one else would. Is this how you repay me?"

Gina burst into tears. "I'm sorry, I'm so sorry..."

Beth held up a hand, silencing them both. "I don't want to hear it. Either of you." She took a deep breath, squaring her shoulders. "Keith, pack your things. I want you out of this house in an hour."

"Beth, be reasonable," Keith pleaded, standing up with the sheet wrapped around his waist. "Where am I supposed to go?"

"Not my problem," Beth spat. She turned to Gina. "You're fired. Don't bother coming in to work tomorrow."

With that, Beth spun on her heel and marched out of the room. She made it halfway down the stairs before the tears came, hot and angry. She gripped the railing her knuckles turning white as she fought to keep her composure.

The sound of hushed arguing drifted down from the bedroom. Beth gritted her teeth and stormed into the kitchen. She grabbed Keith's favorite whiskey from the cabinet and poured herself a generous glass, downing it in one gulp. The alcohol burned her throat, but it was nothing compared to the pain in her chest.

Beth's phone buzzed in her pocket. She pulled it out to see a text from Kelly, her best friend:

Kelly: *"Hey girl, how'd the surprise go? Did Keith love the early Christmas present?"*

A bitter laugh escaped Beth's lips. Oh, he'd gotten an early Christmas present, alright-just not from her.

With shaking fingers, Beth typed out a reply:

Beth :*"Can you come over? I need you."*

Kelly's response was immediate: *"On my way. What's wrong?"*

Beth couldn't bring herself to type out the words. Instead, she sent back a single broken heart emoji.

Upstairs, a door slammed. Beth flinched, then straightened her spine. She wouldn't let them see her cry. Not now.

Footsteps thundered down the stairs. Keith appeared in the kitchen doorway, hastily dressed, with a duffel bag slung over his shoulder. Gina trailed behind him, mascara streaking her cheeks.

"Beth," Keith started, his voice pleading. "Can we please talk about this?"

Beth fixed him with an icy stare. "I think you've done enough."

"It didn't mean anything," he tried again. "It was a mistake."

"A mistake?" Beth's voice was quiet, dangerous. "A mistake is burning cookies or forgetting to set your alarm. This?" She gestured between him and Gina. "This is a choice. You made your choice, Keith. Now live with it."

Gina stepped forward, wringing her hands. "Beth, I'm so sorry. I never meant for this to happen. Please, I need this job..."

"Should have thought of that before you fucked my boyfriend," Beth snapped. "Get out. Both of you."

Keith opened his mouth to argue, but something in Beth's expression made him think better of it. He nodded once, defeated, and headed for the door. Gina followed, her head bowed.

As Keith reached for the doorknob, Beth called out, "Oh, and Keith?" He turned, hope flickering in his eyes. Beth smiled, cold and hard. "Merry Christmas."

The door closed behind them with a final click. Beth stood in the sudden silence, her heart pounding in her ears. Then, as if her strings had been cut, she crumpled to the floor.

Sobs wracked her body, ugly and raw. All the pain and betrayal she'd been holding back came pouring out. She curled into herself, hugging her knees to her chest as she cried.

This wasn't how it was supposed to go. She'd come home early to surprise Keith and celebrate the success of her new holiday menu at her bakery, Sweet Dreams. Now, her relationship was in tatters, and her bakery was short-staffed right before the Christmas rush.

A key turned in the lock, followed by hurried footsteps. "Beth? Honey, where are you?"

Her best friend, Kelly's voice, was like a lifeline. Beth choked out a strangled "Here" between sobs.

Kelly appeared in the kitchen doorway, her blonde hair windswept and her cheeks flushed from the cold. Her blue eyes widened at the sight of Beth on the floor. In an instant, she was by Beth's side, pulling her into a tight hug.

"Oh, sweetie," Kelly murmured, stroking Beth's hair. "What happened?"

Beth buried her face in Kelly's shoulder, her words muffled. "Keith... Gina... They were..."

Understanding dawned on Kelly's face. "That son of a bitch," she hissed. "I'll kill him."

Despite everything, Beth let out a watery chuckle. "Get in line."

Kelly pulled back, cupping Beth's tear-stained face in her hands. "Okay, here's what we're going to do. I'm going to pour us some wine, grab that pint of emergency ice cream I know you have hidden in the freezer, and we're going to talk about what an asshole Keith is. Sound good?"

Beth nodded, sniffling. "Can we add burning his clothes to that list?"

"Honey, we can set his entire wardrobe on fire if that's what you want," Kelly said, helping Beth to her feet. "But first, wine."

As Kelly busied herself in the kitchen, Beth sank onto the couch, feeling drained. She stared at the Christmas tree in the corner, its cheerful lights now seeming to mock her. She and Keith had decorated it together just last week, laughing and stealing kisses as they hung ornaments. Had he been thinking of Gina even then?

Kelly returned with two generous glasses of wine and a pint of chocolate chip cookie dough ice cream. She handed Beth a glass and a spoon before settling beside her on the couch.

"Alright, spill," Kelly said, sipping her wine. "I want all the gory details."

Beth took a long drink, the wine warming her from the inside. "There's not much to tell. I came home early to surprise him. Instead, I found him in bed with Gina."

Kelly's eyebrows shot up. "Gina? As in, your new cashier Gina? The one who can barely count change without using her fingers?"

Beth nodded miserably. "That's the one."

"Oh, honey." Kelly wrapped an arm around Beth's shoulders. "I'm so sorry. What did you do?"

"I kicked them both out," Beth said, stabbing her spoon into the ice cream with perhaps more force than necessary. "Fired Gina on the spot."

Kelly nodded approvingly. "Good. That little home wrecker doesn't deserve your kindness." She paused, then added softly, "Are you okay?"

Beth opened her mouth to say she was fine, but the lie stuck in her throat. Instead, fresh tears welled in her eyes. "No," she whispered. "I'm not okay at all."

Kelly pulled her into another hug, and Beth let herself cry. She cried for the three years she'd invested in a relationship that had crumbled in an instant. She cried for the future she'd imagined with Keith, now nothing more than a fading dream. And she cried for herself, for being so blind, so trusting.

As her sobs subsided, Kelly handed her a tissue. "You know what the worst part is?" Beth said, wiping her eyes. "I feel like such an idiot. How did I not see this coming?"

"Hey, none of that," Kelly said firmly. "You are not an idiot. Keith is the idiot for throwing away the best thing that ever happened to him."

Beth managed a weak smile. "You're biased."

"Damn right I am," Kelly agreed. "And as your biased best friend, it's my duty to remind you that you are amazing. You built Sweet Dreams from the ground up. You make the best damn pastries in all of Upstate New York. And you have curves that most women would kill for."

Beth laughed despite herself. "Now you're just laying it on thick."

"I'm serious!" Kelly insisted. "Beth, you're a catch. And if Keith couldn't see that, then he doesn't deserve you."

Beth sighed, leaning back against the couch. "I know you're right. It's just... we were together for three years, Kel. I thought he was the one. I thought we had a future together."

Kelly squeezed her hand. "I know, sweetie. But maybe this is the universe's way of telling you that there's something better out there for you."

Beth snorted. "What, like my soulmate is just going to fall out of the sky?"

A mischievous glint appeared in Kelly's eye. "Well, maybe not out of the sky. But have you ever considered online dating?"

Beth nearly choked on her wine. "Online dating? Kelly, I just caught my boyfriend cheating on me. The last thing I want to do is jump back into the dating pool."

"Hear me out," Kelly said, holding up a hand. "I'm not saying you need to find your next husband tomorrow. But it might be good for you to put yourself out there. Remind yourself that there are other fish in the sea."

Beth shook her head. "I don't know, Kel. It seems so... impersonal. And what if I end up meeting some creep?"

"That's why you start slow," Kelly explained. "Just chat online for a while. Get to know someone before you even think about meeting in person. And who knows? Maybe you'll connect with someone who makes you forget all about stupid Keith."

Beth bit her lip, considering. The idea of opening herself up to someone new was terrifying. But the alternative-wallowing in misery over Keith—wasn't much better.

"I'll think about it," she said finally.

Kelly beamed. "That's my girl. Now, how about we finish this ice cream and work on our Keith voodoo doll?"

Beth laughed, feeling lighter than she had all evening. "You're ridiculous. But I love you for it."

"I love you too, sweetie," Kelly said, clinking her wine glass against Beth's. "And trust me, this is just the beginning of a new chapter for you. The best is yet to come."

Beth allowed herself to hope as they settled in for a night of wine, ice cream, and Keith-bashing Maybe Kelly was right. Maybe this was the start of something new. And maybe, just maybe, there was someone out there who would love her the way she deserved to be loved.

Two

♥

The pre-dawn chill nipped at Beth's nose as she fumbled with the bakery keys. The glow of the streetlights made Stanford's main street look like a fairytale winter landscape. On any other day, she might have admired it. Today, she just wanted to lose herself in work.

The bell above the door chimed as she entered Sweet Dreams. She flicked on the lights, illuminating the cozy space she'd poured her heart and soul into for the past five years. The familiar scent of sugar and vanilla enveloped her like a warm hug.

"Okay, ladies," Beth muttered to herself, eyeing the industrial mixers. *"Let's dance."*

She cranked up the radio, letting the upbeat Christmas tunes wash over her as she tied on her favorite polka-dot apron. Soon, the kitchen was a whirlwind of activity. Flour dusted her cheeks, and butter smeared her forearms as she kneaded, rolled, and shaped with a feverish intensity.

By the time the sun peeked over the horizon, trays of cookies lined every available surface. Gingerbread men posed jauntily next to delicate snowflake sugar cookies. Chewy chocolate chip cookies nestled against crisp almond biscotti. The air was thick with the aroma of cinnamon, nutmeg, and freshly brewed coffee.

The bell chimed again. Beth looked up to see Reese, her assistant manager, frozen in the doorway, her eyes wide open.

"Holy sugar rush, Batman!" Reese exclaimed, taking in the cookie explosion. "Did Santa's elves break in overnight?"

Beth managed a weak smile. "Couldn't sleep. Thought I'd get a head start on the day."

Reese's expression softened as she hung up her coat. "Rough night?"

"You could say that" Beth sighed, brushing a stray curl from her forehead. "Keith and I... we're done."

"What?" Reese gasped. "But I thought... Oh, Beth, I'm so sorry."

Beth waved off her sympathy, not ready to rehash the details. "It's fine. I'm fine. Everything's fine."

Reese raised an eyebrow, gesturing at the cookie mountain. "Yeah, you look fine. Totally fine. This is exactly what 'fine' looks like."

Despite herself, Beth let out a small chuckle. "Okay, maybe I'm stress-baking a little."

"A little?" Reese snorted. "Honey, this isn't stress-baking. This is a full-on pastry panic attack."

Beth's shoulders slumped. "Is it that obvious?"

Reese draped her arm around Beth's tense shoulders. "You know," she began, a playful edge to her tone, "not everyone can whip up a perfect buttercream frosting while avoiding their own emotional turmoil."

Beth sighed; her gaze distant. Reese softened her voice further and inquired, "Care to share what's eating you?"

Beth hesitated before opening her mouth, intending to deflect with a curt 'no.' But instead of the dismissal she had planned, the words tumbled out of her in an unexpected confessional. "I... I found Keith in bed with Gina."

Reese blinked at this revelation, surprise etching lines on her face. "Wait...new Gina? Our Gina?"

Beth nodded miserably. "Yes, and she was... she was on all fours." The words hung heavy in the air.

A multitude of emotions played across Reese's face - shock giving way to indignation, then morphing into a fierce protective glare as she processed Beth's painful disclosure.

"That two-timing, bottom-feeding, scum-sucking--" Reese's creative string of insults was cut short by the tinkling of the bell.

Mayor Judy Winters bustled in, a whirlwind of tinsel-trimmed enthusiasm. "Good morning, my dears! Oh my, it smells divine in here!"

Beth hastily wiped her eyes, plastering on a smile. "Good morning, Mayor Winters. What brings you by so early?"

The mayor's eyes twinkled. "Why, the most exciting news! The town council has just approved my proposal for Stanford's first-ever Christmas Baking Spectacular!"

Reese and Beth exchanged glances. "Christmas Baking Spectacular?" Reese echoed.

"Yes, isn't it marvelous?" Mayor Winters clapped her hands together. "A grand competition to crown Stanford's best baker. The whole town will be there. And of course," she winked at Beth, "we're all expecting big things from our very own Sweet Dreams."

Beth's mind whirled. A baking competition was the last thing she needed right now. But as she opened her mouth to decline, she caught sight of Keith's favorite cinnamon rolls in the display case. Anger flared in her chest. She'd show him what he was missing.

"Count us in," Beth declared, squaring her shoulders.

Mayor Winters beamed. "Wonderful! I'll put you down as our first official entry. Oh, this is going to be such fun!"

As the mayor swept out in a cloud of peppermint-scented perfume, Reese turned to Beth. "Are you sure about this? You've got a lot on your plate already."

Beth nodded, a determined glint in her eye. "I'm sure. This is exactly what I need. A project to focus on, a goal to work towards."

"Well, if you're in, I'm in," Reese grinned. "Operation Dough-mination is a go!"

They high fived, laughing, only to be interrupted by another chime of the bell. Jessie, Beth's scientist friend, poked her head in.

"Hey, is this a bad time? I smell cookies, and my lab report can totally wait."

Beth waved her in. "Perfect timing. We need your big brain."

As Beth explained the baking competition, Jessie's eyes lit up. "Ooh, this is so exciting! You know, we could approach this scientifically. Optimize your recipe for maximum flavor impact and textural appeal."

Reese blinked. "I understood about half those words, but I'm intrigued."

Jessie was already scribbling equations on a napkin. "See, if we adjust the sugar-to-fat ratio and experiment with different leavening agents..."

Beth and Reese shared an amused look as Jessie rambled on about molecular gastronomy and flavor profiling.

"Jess," Beth interrupted gently. "This all sounds fascinating, but maybe we could start with something simpler? Like, say, which of these cookie recipes tastes best?"

Jessie looked up, a smudge of ink on her nose. "Oh, right. Yes, that works too. We'll need a diverse sample group, and a rating system..."

"Or we could just eat a bunch of cookies," Reese suggested.

"That's basically what I said," Jessie nodded seriously.

As they dove into the great cookie taste test, Beth felt a warmth in her chest that had nothing to do with the oven. This was what she needed—not a man, but her friends, her passion, and a challenge to sink her teeth into.

The rest of the morning flew by in a whirl of customers, coffee, and Christmas carols. By the time the lunch rush died down, Beth was exhausted, but content. She'd just finished boxing up an order when her phone pinged.

Kelly: *How you holding up, sugar plum?*

Beth smiled, tapping out a reply:

Beth: *Better. Busy day at the bakery. Might have accidentally entered a town-wide baking competition.*

Kelly's response was immediate:

Kelly: *That's my girl! Hey, speaking of sweet things, have you thought any more about my suggestion?*

Beth frowned.

Kelly: *Online dating, remember? Your soulmate could be just a click away!*

Beth rolled her eyes but hesitated. Maybe it was the sugar high or the lingering Christmas spirit, but suddenly, the idea didn't seem so crazy.

Beth: *Fine. But if I end up on a date with an axe murderer, I'm blaming you.*

Kelly: *That's the spirit! I'm sending you a link. Trust me, this site is perfect for you.*

Moments later, Beth's phone lit up with a notification. She clicked the link, raising an eyebrow at the site's name: "A Foreign Affair."

"International romance?" she muttered. "Kelly, what are you getting me into?"

But as she scrolled through the profiles of men from around the world, she felt a tiny spark of excitement. This was crazy. This was reckless. This was... exactly what she needed.

Taking a deep breath, Beth clicked "Create Profile."

Name: *Beth Mason*

Age: *32*

Occupation: *Baker and small business owner*

Interests: *Baking (obviously), reading, movies, exploring new cuisines*

She hesitated over the "About Me" section. How do you sum up a person in a few sentences? Finally, she typed:

Just a small-town girl with flour in her hair and sugar in her veins. Looking for someone who can handle my sweet tooth and my sassy mouth. Bonus points if you can knead dough or frost a cupcake!

Before she could second-guess herself, Beth hit "Submit." Her phone pinged almost immediately.

You have a new message!

Heart racing, Beth opened it.

From: *Yuri_V*

Subject: *Privet from Belarus!*

Hello Beth! I couldn't resist messaging when I saw you were a baker. I used to run a nightclub, and let me tell you, nothing sobers up drunk patrons like a good pastry. Any chance you deliver internationally?

Cheers,

Yuri

Beth found herself grinning at the screen. Maybe, just maybe, this wasn't such a bad idea after all.

As she began to type her reply, the bell chimed again. Beth looked up to see Zack from The Daily Grind, the local café, walking in with his usual calm smile.

"Hey, Beth! Got a minute? I had some ideas for a holiday coffee blend, thought you might want to partner up..."

Beth nodded, only half-listening as she finished her message to Yuri. For the first time since last night, she felt a flutter of excitement in her stomach. It wasn't much—just a tiny spark—but it was there.

A sweet new start, indeed.

Three

♥

Yuri's fingers hovered over the keyboard, a half-empty bottle of kvass at his elbow. The soft light from the computer screen illuminated his cozy Minsk apartment. The walls were decorated with worn nightclub posters. Outside, the snow fell softly, blanketing the city in white.

He squinted at the dating profile on his screen, the corners of his mouth tugging upward. Beth Mason, 32, baker from New York. Her smile was warm, her red curls wild and inviting. But it was her bio that had him chuckling.

"Just a small-town girl with flour in her hair and sugar in her veins," he read aloud, his accent wrapping around the words. "Looking for someone who can handle my sweet tooth and my sassy mouth. Bonus points if you can knead dough or frost a cupcake!"

Yuri cracked his knuckles, grinning. "Challenge accepted, moye solnyshko."

He hit reply, fingers flying across the keys:

Dear Beth,

Privet from snowy Minsk! I hope this message finds you well and that you are not buried under a mountain of holiday orders. Your profile caught my eye–not many bakers in the nightclub scene, I must say.

Though perhaps that's where I went wrong. Nothing sobers up drunk patrons like a good pastry, am I right?

I'm curious, what's your signature bake? I'm partial to medovik myself, though I doubt my babushka would approve of my attempt. Let's just say my talents lie more in mixing drinks than mixing dough.

Looking forward to hearing from you,

Yuri

He hit send before he could overthink it, then leaned back in his chair, running a hand through his hair. What was he doing? Online dating? International online dating, no less. His best friend Nik would have a field day with this.

As if summoned by the thought, Yuri's phone buzzed. Speak of the devil.

"Da?" Yuri answered.

"Tell me you're not still moping in your apartment," Nik's voice crackled through the speaker. "It's Friday night, for God's sake."

Yuri glanced at the clock. 11:00 p.m. At one time, he'd just be starting his night at this hour. Now, he was in his pajamas, scrolling through dating sites. How the mighty had fallen.

"I'm not moping," he defended weakly. "I'm... networking."

Nik snorted. "Right. And I'm a Russian prince. Come on, I'm outside. We're going out."

"Nik, I'm not really in the mood—"

"Wasn't asking, Your Highness. You've got five minutes before I sing Vysotsky at the top of my lungs. Your neighbors will love that."

The line went dead. Yuri stared at his phone, torn between annoyance and amusement. That was his best friend, Nik–stubborn as a mule and twice as loud. With a resigned sigh, Yuri stood up to change. Maybe a night out wouldn't be so bad.

Just then, a 'ping' from his computer made him pause. A new message. From Beth.

Yuri's heart did a little skip as he sat back down, opening the message:

Beth: *Hey there, International Man of Mystery!*

Greetings from not-so-snowy Stanford! (That's in New York, by the way. Not the fancy university one.) I'm impressed—most guys lead with a cheesy pick-up line, but you went straight for the baked goods. A man after my own heart!

To answer your question, my signature bake changes with my mood. Today, it's "My-Boyfriend-Cheated-So-I-Stress-Baked-100-Cookies" chocolate chip. Tomorrow, who knows? Maybe "I-Entered-A-Baking-Competition-What-Was-I-Thinking" sourdough?

Medovik, huh? Color me intrigued. I might need that recipe... for research purposes, of course. And hey, mixing drinks is an art form, too. Maybe we could trade skills sometime? I'll teach you to frost; you teach me to flambe. (Is that a thing bartenders do, or am I thinking of fancy chefs?)

Your turn, Mr. Minsk. What's your story? How does one go from running a nightclub to browsing international dating sites? I sense there's a tale there...

Sweetly yours,

Beth

P.S. What's a babushka? Is that like a balaclava? Because if so, I agree. Nobody looks good baking in a ski mask.

Yuri found himself laughing out loud, Nik and his threats of public singing forgotten. He cracked his knuckles, ready to reply, when his phone buzzed again. This time, it was accompanied by the distant strains of "Koni Priveredlivye" floating up from the street.

Torn, Yuri glanced between his phone and the computer. The responsible thing would be to go out with his friend. To try and recapture some of his old life.

"Yuri!" Nik's voice carried through the open window. "I'm on verse two! Don't make me do the whole song!"

With a groan, Yuri made his decision. He quickly typed out a response to Beth:

Yuri: *Apologies, moye solnyshko, but duty calls. My friend is threatening to serenade the entire block if I don't join him for a night out. Raincheck on that fascinating story and cultural exchange? I promise it's worth the wait.*

Sleep sweet, Baker Beth. Dream of sugar plums... or whatever it is you baker's dream of.

Dosvidaniya for now,

Yuri

P.S. Babushka = grandmother. Balaclava = definitely not recommended for baking. Or anything, really. Unless you're robbing a bank in Siberia.

He hit send, then hurried to change. By the time he made it downstairs, Nik was on verse four, much to the dismay of Yuri's elderly neighbors.

"Alright, alright, I'm here," Yuri grumbled, shoving his hands in his pockets. "You can stop torturing everyone now."

Nik grinned, slinging an arm around Yuri's shoulders. "Aw, you love my singing. Admit it."

"I'd rather admit to tax fraud," Yuri retorted, but there was no heat in it. Despite his reluctance, he felt a familiar thrill of anticipation. A night out with Nik was never dull.

As they walked towards their favorite bar, Nik studied his friend. "So, what's her name?"

Yuri nearly tripped over his own feet. "What? Who?"

"The girl. The one that had you 'networking' instead of answering my calls."

"There's no girl," Yuri protested too quickly.

Nik's grin widened. "Uh-huh. And that's why you're blushing like a schoolboy. Come on, spill. Is she Russian? Please tell me she's not another dancer. I can't handle another Natasha situation."

Yuri winced at the memory. "She's not a dancer. She's... she's a baker. From America."

Nik stopped dead in his tracks. "A baker. From America," he repeated slowly. "Yuri, tell me you're not on one of those international dating sites."

Yuri's silence was answer enough.

"Bozhe moy," Nik groaned. "Have you learned nothing from those crime documentaries I made you watch? She's probably a 50-year-old man named Chuck who wants to steal your kidneys!"

"She's not—" Yuri started to argue, then caught himself. "Look, it's not serious. We just started chatting. She seems... nice."

"Nice," Nik echoed. "Right. Well, when you wake up in a bathtub full of ice, don't come crying to me."

Despite his words, Nik's tone was more concerned than mocking. Yuri felt a surge of affection for his friend. "I promise to keep both my kidneys intact," he said solemnly. "Now, are we going to drink or what?"

People filled the crowded bar, smoke filled the air, and laughter echoed throughout. Yuri breathed it in, feeling a familiar ache. It wasn't Rhapsody, his beloved lost nightclub, but it was close.

As Nik ordered their usual vodkas, Yuri's mind wandered back to Beth. He found himself wondering what she was doing now –

Neither of them noticed the hours slipping by, lost in their own private world. It wasn't until Beth's oven timer went off that they realized they'd been talking for nearly three hours.

"Oh shoot," Beth said reluctantly. "I've got to go. The bakery awaits."

Yuri nodded, fighting his disappointment. "Of course. Go, create sweet miracles."

Beth hesitated before blurting out, "Can we do this again?"

Yuri's heart leapt. "Da. Yes. Tomorrow?"

"Tomorrow," Beth agreed, her smile was radiant. "It's a date. I mean, not a date-date, but... you know what I mean."

"I know," Yuri whispered. "Dosvidaniya, Baker Beth."

"Goodbye, Yuri from Minsk."

As the screen went dark, Yuri leaned back in his chair, a foolish grin on his face. He was in trouble. Deep, sweet trouble.

His phone buzzed. Nik again.

Nik; *"So? How are your kidneys?"*

Yuri chuckled, typing back:

Yuri: *"Intact. But I think I might be losing something else."*

In Stanford, Beth hummed as she prepared for the day, her steps light despite her lack of sleep. For the first time since the Keith disaster, she felt a flutter of hope.

Her phone chimed. A message from Kelly:

Kelly: *"Well? How's the international manhunt going?"*

Beth smiled, responding:

Beth: *"Let's just say... things are heating up. And not just the ovens."*

As she tied on her apron, Beth looked forward to more than just baking for the first time in days. She had a video call to prepare for, after all. And maybe, just maybe, a whole new recipe for happiness to discover.

Four

♥

Beth's fingers flew across her phone screen, a smile playing on her lips as she typed:

Beth: *"So, Mr. International, what's on your agenda today? More vodka-fueled serenades, or are you planning to single-handedly revive the Soviet disco scene?"*

She hit send, then returned her attention to the mountain of dough before her. The kitchen of Sweet Dreams was a whirlwind of activity, the air thick with the scent of cinnamon and vanilla. Christmas was three weeks away, and the orders were piling up faster than snow in a blizzard.

Her phone pinged. Beth wiped her hands on her apron and reached for it, her heart skipping a little.

Yuri: *"Alas, my disco days are behind me. My bell bottoms tragically shrunk in the wash. Today, I'm drowning my sorrows in paperwork. Exciting, da?"*

Beth chuckled, quickly typing back:

Beth: *"Ooh, paperwork. Sexy. Don't let all that power go to your head, now."*

"Beth? Earth to Beth!" Reese's voice cut through her Yuri-induced haze. "The timer's been going off for, like, a full minute. Unless you're aiming for 'Charcoal Chic' as our new flavor..."

"Shit!" Beth yelped, dropping her phone and rushing to the oven. She yanked it open, a plume of smoke escaping. Coughing, she pulled out a tray of what were once perfectly formed gingerbread men, now resembling tiny, burned corpses.

"Well," Reese said, peering over her shoulder, "look on the bright side. If the whole 'Christmas Baking Spectacular' thing doesn't work out, we could always pivot to Halloween treats."

Beth groaned, dumping the charred cookies into the trash. "Hilarious. God, what is wrong with me lately? I never burn things."

Reese's eyes twinkled knowingly. "Uh-huh. And I'm sure it has nothing to do with a certain international man of mystery you've been texting non-stop for the past week."

Beth felt her cheeks heat up. "I don't know what you're talking about," she mumbled, busying herself with preparing a new batch of dough.

"Oh please," Reese scoffed. "You've been walking around with this goofy grin on your face, checking your phone every two seconds. Spill, boss lady. Who is he?"

Beth sighed, knowing resistance was futile. "His name is Yuri. He's from Belarus. We met on that dating site Kelly signed me up for."

Reese's eyebrows shot up. "Belarus? Isn't that like, Dracula territory?"

"That's Transylvania," Beth corrected, rolling her eyes. "Belarus is... actually, I'm not entirely sure where it is. Near Russia, I think?"

"Ooh, mysterious," Reese waggled her eyebrows. "So, what's he like? Is he dreamy? Does he have an accent? Tell me everything!"

Beth couldn't help but smile. "He's... different. Funny, smart. He used to run this amazing nightclub in Minsk. And yes, he has an accent. It's... kind of incredible."

"Sounds like someone's got a crush," Reese sing songed. "When are you going to meet him in person?"

The smile slipped from Beth's face. "I don't know if we will. He's there, I'm here. It's just... fun. For now."

Reese attempted to respond, but the chime of the bakery door interrupted her. Zack from The Daily Grind walked in with a tray of coffee cups.

"Ladies," he greeted with a grin. "I come bearing gifts. Thought you might need a caffeine boost."

"You're a lifesaver, Zack," Beth said, gratefully accepting a cup. She took a sip and frowned. "This isn't your usual blend."

Zack's eyes lit up. "Good catch! It's a new holiday special I'm working on. Peppermint mocha with a hint of... can you guess?"

Beth took another sip, considering. "Cinnamon?"

"Close," Zack said. "It's actually—"

Beth's phone pinged again. She glanced at it reflexively.

Yuri: *"Power? Ha! The only thing going to my head is the fumes from all this ink. Save me, moye solnyshko. Tell me a sweet story. Preferably one involving less paperwork and more frosting."*

Beth bit her lip to keep from grinning like an idiot.

"Um, Beth?" Zack's voice brought her back to reality. "You okay there?"

"What? Oh, yeah. Sorry, Zack. You were saying? About the coffee?"

Zack's smile dimmed slightly. "Right. It's star anise. Adds a subtle licorice note. I was thinking maybe we could collaborate on a coffee-flavored holiday cookie to go with it?"

"That sounds great," Beth said, already texting a reply to Yuri.

Beth: *"Once upon a time, there was a dashing baker who tragically burnt her gingerbread men to a crisp because a charming foreigner distracted her. The end. Moral of the story? Texting and baking don't mix."*

"So, what do you think?" Zack asked, looking at her expectantly.

Beth blinked. "About what?"

Zack's brow furrowed. "The cookie collaboration? For the Christmas market?"

"Oh! Right. Yes, definitely. Let's set up a time to brainstorm. Maybe next week?"

Zack nodded, but he was eyeing her curiously. "Everything okay, Beth? You seem a little... distracted."

Beth forced a bright smile. "Everything's great! Just busy with holiday orders, you know how it is."

Her phone pinged again. Beth's hand twitched towards it, but she resisted. Zack didn't look entirely convinced, but he let it go.

"Alright, well, I'll let you get back to it. Let me know when you want to get together for that brainstorming session."

Beth snatched up her phone as soon as the door closed behind him.

Yuri: *"Ah, the tragic tale of the Gingerbread Massacre. I weep for their little cookie souls. Perhaps we should hold a memorial? I'll bring the vodka; you bring the frosting. We can give them a proper send-off."*

Beth giggled, earning a pointed look from Reese.

"What?" Beth defended. "He's funny!"

Reese shook her head, amused. "Uh-huh. You know, for someone who's 'just having fun,' you're awfully smitten."

Beth opened her mouth to argue, then closed it. Was she smitten? The thought was both thrilling and terrifying.

Her phone buzzed again, this time with an incoming video call. Yuri's name flashed on the screen. Beth's heart did a little flip.

"I, uh, need to take this," she said to Reese. "In my office. For... business reasons."

Reese snorted. "Right. 'Business.' Have fun with your 'business call,' boss."

Beth stuck out her tongue childishly, then hurried to her tiny office in the back. She closed the door, took a deep breath, and answered the call.

Yuri's face filled the screen, his blue eyes crinkling as he smiled. "Privet, moye solnyshko. I hope I'm not interrupting your great gingerbread revival?"

Beth laughed, settling into her chair. "You're safe. The great gingerbread massacre of 2024 is behind us. We're in full recovery mode now."

"Excellent news," Yuri nodded solemnly. "I was worried I'd have to organize a rescue mission. Although," he leaned in, "I wouldn't mind swooping in to save the day. I've always wanted to be a hero."

"My hero," Beth said dramatically, placing a hand over her heart. Then, dropping the act, "So, what's up? Shouldn't you be drowning in paperwork right now?"

Yuri groaned, running a hand through his hair. "I needed a break. One can only read so many legal documents before one's eyes start to cross. Besides," he added with a wink, "I much prefer looking at you."

Beth felt her cheeks warm. "Flatterer. I'll have you know I'm a mess. I'm covered in flour, my hair's a disaster, and I smell like burnt cookies."

"Sounds perfect," Yuri murmured.

There was a moment of charged silence, filled with things unsaid. Beth's heart raced. This was dangerous territory.

"So," she said brightly, breaking the tension. "Tell me more about this paperwork. Anything exciting? Any deep, dark secrets of the Belarusian nightclub scene?"

Yuri chuckled. "Alas, no. Just boring legal stuff. I'm trying to settle some final accounts from Rhapsody."

Beth's smile faded. She knew how much the loss of his club still hurt him. "I'm sorry, Yuri. That must be tough."

He shrugged, but she could see the sadness in his eyes. "It is what it is. But enough about my troubles. Tell me about your day, moye solnyshko. Any more baking disasters I should know about?"

As Beth launched into a detailed account of her morning, complete with dramatic reenactments of the Great Gingerbread Tragedy, she felt a warm glow in her chest. It was so easy with Yuri, so natural. Like they'd known each other for years instead of days.

Their conversation flowed effortlessly, from baking to music to childhood memories. Beth found herself sharing stories she'd never told anyone, not even Kelly. And Yuri listened, really listened, his eyes warm and attentive.

It wasn't until Reese knocked on the office door that Beth realized an hour had passed.

"Boss? Sorry to interrupt your, uh, 'business call,' but we've got a situation out here. Mrs. Klaus is demanding her usual order but with a 'festive twist.' Whatever that means."

Beth groaned. "I'll be right there!" To Yuri, she said apologetically, "Duty calls. Raincheck?"

"Always," Yuri smiled. "Go save Christmas, Baker Beth. I'll be here, drowning in paperwork and dreaming of gingerbread."

As Beth ended the call and hurried out to deal with the latest crisis, she couldn't shake the feeling that something had shifted. This thing with Yuri, whatever it was, was quickly becoming more than just fun.

It was becoming real. And that was both exciting and terrifying.

But as she plastered on a smile and prepared to face Mrs. Klaus and her demands for 'festive twists,' Beth realized something. She looked forward to tomorrow for the first time since the Keith debacle. And the day after that. And the day after that.

All because of a charming Belarusian with a killer accent and a knack for making her laugh.

Maybe, just maybe, this Christmas would be sweet after all.

Five

♥

The kitchen of Sweet Dreams was a full of chaos. Mixers whirred, ovens dinged, and in the center of it all, Beth pirouetted between workstations like a sugar-dusted ballerina.

"Reese!" she called over her shoulder, "How's that gingerbread house coming along?"

Reese, up to her elbows in royal icing, grimaced. "Let's just say it's more 'Leaning Tower of Pisa' than 'winter wonderland' right now."

Beth suppressed a laugh. "Well, as long as it's structurally sound enough to—"

The cheerful chime of the bakery's bell cut her off. Zack strolled in, a paper bag in one hand and a tray of coffee cups in the other.

"Ladies," he grinned, "I come bearing gifts. Thought you might need a pick-me-up."

"Zack," Beth breathed, "you're a lifesaver." She grabbed a cup, inhaling deeply. "Is this the new blend we talked about?"

Zack nodded eagerly. "Yep! Cinnamon and star anise."

Beth took a sip, her eyes widening. "Zack, this is even better than the first batch you brought us."

Her phone buzzed in her apron pocket. Beth's heart did a little flip as she saw Yuri's name on the screen.

Yuri: *"Dobroye utro, moye solnyshko! Quick question: is it normal to dream about drowning in a sea of gingerbread men? Asking for a friend. The friend is me. I may be spending too much time thinking about your baking adventures."*

Beth bit her lip to keep from grinning like an idiot.

"Beth?" Zack's voice brought her back to reality. "Everything okay?"

"What? Oh, yeah. Sorry." She gestured with the coffee cup. "This is great, Zack. It's such a unique blend. I love it."

Zack beamed. "Thanks! I brought some ideas over for the collaboration." He held up the paper bag.

Just then, Beth's phone buzzed again. She glanced at it reflexively.

Yuri: *"Also, unrelated, but how do you feel about mustaches? Considering growing one. Could be dashing, no?"*

Beth snorted, then quickly tried to cover it with a cough when Zack looked at her quizzically.

"Sorry," she said, "throat tickle. You were saying? About the coffee treats?"

Zack's brow furrowed slightly. "Right. Well, I was thinking maybe some mocha macarons? Or espresso brownies?"

Beth nodded absently, her fingers already tapping out a reply to Yuri.

Beth: *"Gingerbread dreams, huh? Sounds like a sweet nightmare to me. As for the mustache... let's just say I prefer my men clean-shaven and Eastern European. "*

She hit send, then looked up to find Zack staring at her expectantly. "Oh! Um, those both sound great. Why don't we set up a time to experiment next week?"

Zack opened his mouth to respond, but a crash from the front of the bakery interrupted him, followed by Reese's muffled curse.

"Shoot," Beth muttered. "Zack, I'm so sorry, but I should probably..."

"No worries," Zack said, though his smile seemed a bit forced. "I'll just leave these samples here. Let me know when you want to get together."

As Zack headed out, Reese poked her head around the corner, a smear of icing on her cheek. "So, that was awkward."

Beth frowned, helping Reese clean up the remains of what appeared to be a gingerbread apocalypse. "What do you mean?"

Reese rolled her eyes. "Oh, come on. Zack was totally trying to ask you out, and you were too busy sexting your European boyfriend to notice."

"What? No, he wasn't. And I wasn't sexting!" Beth protested, her cheeks warming. "Yuri and I are just friends."

"Uh-huh," Reese smirked. "Friends who make you blush like a teenager and ignore cute, available local guys. Got it."

Before Beth could argue further, the bakery door chimed again. This time, it was Jessie, looking frazzled and carrying what appeared to be a small chemistry set.

"Beth!" she exclaimed, "I've had a breakthrough! I think I've found a way to stabilize the molecular structure of your sugar cookies to prevent spreading during baking while maintaining optimal chewiness!"

Beth blinked, trying to process this. "That's... great, Jess. But why do you have a Bunsen burner?"

Jessie waved her hand dismissively. "Oh, that's for the caramelization experiment. But forget that for now. We need to run some tests on your dough. Where's your kitchen scale? And do you have any liquid nitrogen?"

Reese sidled up to Beth, whispering, "Ten bucks says she blows something up within the hour."

Beth elbowed her but couldn't help grinning. "Now, now. Jessie's ideas might be a little... unconventional, but they're always interesting."

Beth's phone buzzed again as Jessie set up her impromptu lab on one of the free counters, chattering excitedly about glucose molecules and heat distribution.

Yuri: *"Clean-shaven and Eastern European, eh? Well, lucky for you, I fit that bill perfectly. Though I must say, I'm a little hurt. I think I could rock a mustache. Very Freddie Mercury, no?"*

Beth giggled, quickly typing back,

Beth: *"Freddie Mercury, huh? Bold choice. Though I suppose if anyone could pull it off, it'd be you. But let's not test that theory, shall we? I like your face just as it is."*

"Earth to Beth!" Reese's voice cut through her Yuri-induced haze. "Your cookie scientist is about to set fire to our sugar supply."

"What? Jessie, no!" Beth yelped, rushing over to where Jessie was indeed attempting to caramelize sugar with her Bunsen burner. "We have blowtorches for that!"

As Beth attempted to save her bakery from becoming a science experiment gone wrong, her phone pinged again. She resisted the urge to check it immediately, but her resolve lasted all of thirty seconds.

Yuri: *"You like my face, eh? High praise indeed from a master of sweet things. Perhaps I should send you a picture, just to remind you what you're missing?"*

Beth's heart raced. *Was he flirting? Were they flirting?* Before she could overthink it, she snapped a quick selfie–flour on her cheek, hair a mess, grinning like a fool–and sent it with the caption:

"Only if you return the favor, Mr. Minsk. Though I warn you, this is what "death by chocolate" looks like."

"Beth!" Jessie's excited voice broke through her trance. "I think I've done it! Come look at these cookies!"

Beth tucked her phone away, turning to see Jessie proudly displaying a tray of perfectly uniform, golden-brown cookies. They looked impressive; Beth had to admit.

"Wow, Jess. These look great. How do they taste?"

Jessie's triumphant smile faltered. "Oh. I, uh, I didn't actually try them. I was too focused on the structural integrity and surface-area-to-volume ratio to try them."

Reese snorted. "Only you would forget the most important part of a cookie–eating it!"

Beth felt her phone buzz again as the three women sampled Jessie's scientifically perfect (if slightly bland) cookies. She resisted for thirty seconds before excusing herself to check it.

Her breath caught as Yuri's image filled her screen. He was in what looked like an office, his hair slightly mussed, a five o'clock shadow darkening his jaw. He was smiling that crooked smile that made her knees weak, even though a screen.

The caption read: *Death by chocolate looks good on you, moye solnyshko. Though I must say, "death by paperwork" is significantly less attractive.*

Beth felt a warmth spread through her chest that had nothing to do with the ovens. She was in trouble, she realized. Deep, sweet trouble.

"Beth?" Reese's voice floated from the kitchen. "Not to interrupt your virtual make-out session, but we've got a situation out here. Mrs. Klaus is back, and she's demanding edible glitter. I don't even know if that's a real thing!"

Beth groaned, reluctantly putting her phone away. "Coming!" she called back. To Yuri, she quickly typed:

Beth: *"Duty calls. Apparently, I need to make glitter edible. Just another day in the life of a small-town baker. Talk later?"*

His reply was almost instant:

Yuri; *"Always, moye solnyshko. Go sprinkle your magic. I'll be here, drowning in paperwork and dreaming of sparkling cookies... and the beautiful baker who makes them."*

As Beth returned to the chaos of her kitchen, a smile playing on her lips, she couldn't help but think that maybe, just maybe, this Christmas would be her sweetest yet.

Six

B eth stared at her phone, thumb hovering over the 'send' button. The message read:

Beth: *"So... hypothetically speaking, how would you feel about a surprise visit from a certain American baker? Asking for a friend. The friend is me. I may be losing my mind."*

She groaned, deleting the text for the fifth time. What was she thinking? She'd known Yuri for all of two weeks. Flying to Belarus for a week was insane. Right?

A knock on her front door startled her out of her daydream. She opened it to find Mrs. Klaus, her elderly neighbor, holding a plate of cookies.

"Beth, dear! I thought you might need a pick-me-up. You've seemed a bit... distracted lately."

Beth accepted the plate with a weak smile. "Thanks, Mrs. Klaus. That's really thoughtful of you."

Mrs. Klaus peered at her over her glasses. "Boy troubles?"

Beth blinked. "What? No, I—how did you...?"

The older woman chuckled. "Honey, I've been around the block a few times. I know that look. So, who is he? That nice cafe owner? What was his name... Zack?"

"No, it's not Zack," Beth sighed, ushering Mrs. Klaus inside. "It's... complicated."

Mrs. Klaus settled onto the couch, patting the spot next to her. "Well, then. Uncomplicate it for me."

Beth sat, running a hand through her unruly curls. "His name is Yuri. He's from Belarus. We met online and... I think I'm falling for him."

Mrs. Klaus's eyebrows shot up. "Belarus? My, my. That's quite a distance."

"I know," Beth groaned. "It's crazy, right? I mean, I've never even met him in person. But when we talk, it's like... like..."

"Like coming home?" Mrs. Klaus supplied softly.

Beth nodded, surprised at the accuracy of the description.

Mrs. Klaus patted her hand. "Love doesn't always make sense, dear. Sometimes, it's just a feeling. A knowing. The question is, what are you going to do about it?"

Before Beth could respond, her phone buzzed. Yuri's face lit up the screen, a video call incoming. Beth's heart did a little flip.

"Speaking of the devil," Mrs. Klaus winked. "Go on, answer it. I'll see myself out. But Beth?" She paused at the door. "Don't let fear stop you from chasing happiness. Even if it's halfway across the world."

With that advice, she left. Beth took a deep breath and answered the call.

"Privet, moye solnyshko!" Yuri's cheerful voice filled the room. "I hope I'm not interrupting anything important. Like a top-secret cookie experiment. Or a heated debate about the merits of sprinkles versus chocolate chips."

Beth couldn't help but smile. "Nope, no cookie emergencies at the moment. Although I did just have a rather cryptic conversation with my neighbor about chasing happiness across continents."

Yuri's eyebrows rose. "Oh? And what brought on this intercontinental discussion?"

Beth felt her cheeks warm. "Oh, you know. Just... general life pondering. Nothing specific."

"Uh-huh," Yuri smirked. "And I suppose this pondering has nothing to do with a devilishly handsome Belarusian who's been occupying your thoughts?"

"Devilishly handsome? My, someone's confident," Beth teased, grateful for the shift to lighter territory.

Yuri struck a dramatic pose. "What can I say? It's a curse, really. The burden of being irresistible."

Beth laughed, the tension in her chest easing. This was why she was falling for him. He could make her laugh even when her thoughts were a tangled mess.

"So," Yuri continued, his tone softening. "What's really on your mind, moye solnyshko? You seem... pensive."

Beth sighed, fiddling with a loose thread on her sweater. "I just... I've been thinking about us. About what we're doing here."

Yuri's smile faded slightly. "Having second thoughts?"

"No!" Beth said quickly. "No, not at all. It's just... is this crazy? We've never even met in person. We live on different continents. And yet..."

"And yet?" Yuri prompted gently.

"And yet I've never felt this way about anyone before," Beth admitted softly. "It's scary."

Yuri was quiet for a moment. When he spoke, his voice was low and serious. "I know, Beth. I feel it too. The distance, the uncertainty... it's not easy. But when I talk to you, when I see your smile... nothing else matters."

Beth felt tears prick in her eyes. "Yuri..."

"I have an idea," he said suddenly. "Close your eyes."

Beth raised an eyebrow. "What?"

"Just trust me. Close your eyes."

Feeling a bit foolish, Beth complied.

"Now," Yuri's voice came through the speaker, warm and close. "Imagine I'm there with you. Imagine I'm holding your hand. Can you feel it?"

To her surprise, Beth could almost sense the warmth of his palm against hers. She nodded, not trusting her voice.

"That feeling? That's real, Beth. It doesn't matter if we're in the same room or on opposite sides of the world. What we have is real."

Beth opened her eyes, a tear sliding down her cheek. "How do you always know exactly what to say?"

Yuri grinned. "It's a gift. Along with my devilish good looks, of course."

Beth laughed, wiping her eyes. "Of course. How could I forget?"

Just then, Beth's kitchen timer went off. She groaned. "Ugh, I forgot I had a test batch in the oven. Hold that thought?"

As Beth rushed to salvage her experimental gingerbread, her mind was whirling. Mrs. Klaus's words echoed in her head: "Don't let fear stop you from chasing happiness."

Making a split-second decision, she grabbed her phone and typed out a message to Kelly:

Beth: *"Hey, what are your thoughts on a spontaneous trip to Belarus?"*

Kelly's response was almost immediate:

Kelly: *"Girl, YES! When do we leave? Also, where exactly is Belarus?"*

Laughing, Beth returned to her video call with Yuri. He was humming what sounded suspiciously like "Jingle Bells" in Russian.

"Sorry about that," she said. "Cookie crisis averted."

"Excellent news," Yuri nodded solemnly. "We wouldn't want any innocent gingerbread men to suffer. So, where were we?"

Beth took a deep breath. "Actually, I was thinking... what if we didn't have to imagine?"

Yuri's brow furrowed. "What do you mean?"

"I mean," Beth said, her heart racing, "what if I came to visit you? In Belarus for a week. For Christmas."

Yuri's eyes widened. For a moment, he was silent, and Beth felt her stomach drop. But then, slowly, a grin spread across his face.

"Beth Mason," he said, his voice filled with wonder, "you continue to surprise me. Are you serious?"

Beth nodded, a giddy laugh escaping her. "Completely serious. Totally insane, but serious."

Yuri's laugh joined hers, rich and warm. "Then yes. A thousand times, yes. Come to Belarus, moye solnyshko. Let's make this Christmas one to remember."

As they began excitedly planning her trip, Beth felt a weight lift from her shoulders. She didn't know what the future held, but she knew one thing for certain: this Christmas would be unlike any other.

And she couldn't wait.

Seven

♥

A tornado of fabric surrounded Beth as she stood in front of her closet. Dresses, sweaters, and jeans lay strewn across her bed, a testament to her indecision. Her suitcase sat open, mockingly empty.

"This is hopeless," she groaned, flopping onto the bed. "What does one even wear to seduce a sexy Belarusian?"

Her phone buzzed. Kelly's name flashed on the screen.

Kelly: *"So? Packed yet? Or are you still having a fashion crisis?"*

Beth: *"Definitely crisis mode. Help!"*

Kelly: *"On my way. Bringing reinforcements."*

Fifteen minutes later, Kelly burst through the door, arms laden with shopping bags. Jessie trailed behind, looking slightly overwhelmed.

"Ladies," Kelly announced, "Operation: Belarusian Seduction is officially underway."

Beth laughed, relief flooding through her. "You're a lifesaver, Kel. And Jessie! I didn't expect to see you here."

Jessie shrugged, a slight blush coloring her cheeks. "Kelly said it was an emergency. I thought maybe you'd blown up the kitchen or something."

"Oh honey," Kelly patted Jessie's arm. "This is a much more delicious kind of emergency. Now, let's see what we're working with."

As Kelly dove into the shopping bags, pulling out an array of lacy, silky items, Beth's phone buzzed again. Yuri's name lit up the screen.

Yuri: *"Important question: how do you feel about ice skating? Asking for a friend. The friend is me. I may be planning our first date."*

Beth's heart did a little flip. She quickly typed back:

Beth: *"Ice skating sounds perfect. Fair warning, though, I have all the grace of a newborn giraffe on ice. Hope you know CPR."*

"Ooh, who's that?" Kelly's voice sing-songed from behind her. "Lover boy?"

Beth felt her cheeks warm. "Maybe. He's asking about ice skating."

Kelly's eyes lit up. "Perfect! I packed just the thing." She pulled out a form-fitting sweater dress in a deep emerald green. "Pair this with leggings and boots, and you'll be the hottest thing on ice. You can thank me later."

As Beth admired the dress, her phone buzzed again.

Yuri: *"CPR, eh? Well, I am trained in mouth-to-mouth. Though perhaps we should practice. You know, just to be safe. ;)"*

Beth nearly choked on air. Were they flirting? They were definitely flirting.

"Earth to Beth!" Jessie's voice cut through her Yuri-induced haze. "Your face is turning the color of your hair. Everything okay?"

"What? Oh, yeah. Everything's great," Beth mumbled, quickly typing back:

Beth: *"Practice makes perfect, Mr. Minsk. I'll pencil you in for a thorough lesson. For safety reasons, of course."*

"Alright, spill," Kelly demanded, hands on hips. "What's got you blushing like a virgin on prom night?"

Beth hesitated, then passed her phone to Kelly. Might as well get some expert advice.

Kelly's gaze danced over the texts, a devilish smirk on her lips. "Oh, sweetheart, he's definitely looking for a ticket to ride the Beth Express."

"What? No... we're just...it's just playful chatter," Beth rebutted feebly.

Kelly arched an eyebrow at her friend, a knowing glint in her eye. "Beth, darling, you and Keith have been done for a couple of weeks now. Reminder, all work and no play make for a very dull girl..."

Jessie peered over Kelly's shoulder, her eyebrows rising. "I may not be an expert in flirting, but even I can see this is more than friendly. The winky face alone is highly suggestive."

Beth groaned, burying her face in her hands. "Oh god. What am I doing? I'm flying halfway across the world to meet a man I've only seen through a screen. This is insane, right?"

Kelly sat beside her, wrapping an arm around her shoulders. "Sweetie, love is always a little insane. But from what I've seen, this Yuri guy is crazy about you. And life's too short to play it safe all the time."

"Besides," Jessie added, "statistically speaking, long-distance relationships that transition to in-person meetings have a 58% success rate, which is actually quite promising considering the variables involved."

Beth and Kelly stared at her for a moment before bursting into laughter.

"Thanks, Jess," Beth said, wiping tears of joy from her eyes. "That 's... oddly comforting."

Just then, Beth's phone chimed with an incoming video call from Yuri. She froze, looking panicked.

"Answer it!" Kelly hissed, shoving the phone into Beth's hands.

Taking a deep breath, Beth hit 'accept.' Yuri's face filled the screen, his blue eyes crinkling as he smiled.

"Privet, moye solnyshko! I hope I'm not interrupting anything important."

Beth was suddenly very aware that she was surrounded by lingerie and half-packed suitcases. "Nope! Not interrupting at all. Just, uh, doing some light reading."

Yuri raised an eyebrow, clearly not buying it. "Light reading, eh? Must be quite the page-turner. You're looking a little flushed."

Behind the phone, Kelly made exaggerated kissing faces while Jessie looked on, fascinated.

"Oh, you know," Beth stammered, "just some... steamy romance novels. Gotta stay warm in this winter weather somehow, right?"

Yuri's eyes darkened slightly, his voice dropping an octave. "Well, I can think of a few other ways to stay warm. Perhaps I could demonstrate when you get here."

Beth felt heat pool in her stomach. "I... I'd like that," she managed to say.

A crash from behind her made Beth jump. She turned to see Kelly tangled in a pile of clothes, having apparently tripped in her attempt to eavesdrop more closely.

"Everything okay over there?" Yuri asked, amusement clear in his voice.

"Fine! Everything's fine," Beth said quickly. "Just my, uh, cat. Very clumsy cat."

"I didn't know you had a cat," Yuri said, perplexed.

"Newly adopted," Beth lied smoothly. "She's still adjusting."

Still on the floor, Kelly let out an indignant "meow."

Yuri chuckled. "Well, I should let you get back to your... reading. And cat wrangling. But Beth?"

"Yes?" she breathed.

"I can't wait to see you, in person, to hold you." His voice was low and intimate.

Beth felt a shiver run down her spine. "Me too, Yuri. Soon."

As she ended the call, she turned to find Kelly and Jessie staring at her, Kelly with a triumphant grin and Jessie with a look of scientific fascination.

"Well," Kelly said, standing up and brushing herself off. "I think it's safe to say we need to pack some extra-sexy pajamas. And maybe some mistletoe. Just in case."

As the three women dissolved into giggles and resumed their packing efforts, Beth felt a mix of excitement and nerves flutter in her stomach. In just a few days, she'd be face to face with Yuri. No screens, no distance between them.

Eight

A couple of days later, Beth's heart pounded as she stepped off the plane at Minsk National Airport. The butterflies in her stomach had morphed into full-fledged eagles during the flight. Now, they were threatening to carry her away entirely.

She clutched her carry-on bag, eyes scanning the crowd. And then, suddenly, there he was.

Yuri stood near the arrivals gate, a bouquet of sunflowers in one hand and a sign that read "My American Solnyshko" in the other. His dark hair was slightly tousled, his blue eyes bright with anticipation. He was even more handsome in person, if that was possible.

Their eyes met across the terminal. For a moment, time seemed to stand still.

Then Beth was moving, half-walking, half-running towards him. Yuri's face broke into a wide grin as he opened his arms.

She collided with him, breathing in the scent of his cologne. His arms wrapped around her, strong and sure, and her nerves suddenly melted away. This felt right. This felt like coming home.

"Privet, moye solnyshko," Yuri murmured into her hair. "Welcome to Belarus."

Beth pulled back slightly, looking up at him. "Hi," she breathed, suddenly feeling shy.

Yuri's eyes crinkled as he smiled down at her. "Hi yourself. You know, you're even more beautiful in person. I didn't think that was possible."

Beth felt her cheeks warm. "Flatterer. You're not so bad yourself, Mr. Minsk."

They stood there for a moment, just drinking each other in. Then Yuri seemed to remember the flowers. "Oh! These are for you. I hope you like sunflowers."

"They're perfect," Beth said, accepting the bouquet. "Thank you."

As she buried her nose in the flowers, Yuri reached out and tucked a stray curl behind her ear. The simple touch sent a shiver down her spine.

"So," he said, his voice low and warm, "shall we get out of here? If you're not too jet lagged, I have a whole day planned for us."

Beth nodded eagerly. "Lead the way. I'm running on pure adrenaline and excitement right now."

Yuri chuckled, taking her hand. The warmth of his palm against hers felt electric. "Well then, let's make the most of it. First stop; introducing you to real Belarusian cuisine."

As they made their way out of the airport, Beth couldn't help but notice the appreciative glances Yuri was getting from other women. She felt a mix of pride and possessiveness. This gorgeous man was here with her.

In the taxi, Yuri kept stealing glances at her as if he couldn't quite believe she was real. Beth felt the same way. After weeks of screens and messages, being able to reach out and touch him was almost overwhelming.

"So," Beth said, trying to break the charged silence, "what's on the menu for this culinary adventure?"

Yuri's eyes lit up. "Ah, I thought we'd start with some draniki – potato pancakes. And maybe some machanka, which is a pork stew. Oh, and you have to try our kvass!"

As he enthusiastically described Belarusian cuisine, Beth was captivated not just by his words but also by how his hands moved as he talked, the curve of his lips, and the spark in his eyes.

Suddenly, Yuri paused mid-sentence. "What?" he asked, a slight smirk on his lips. "Do I have something on my face?"

Beth realized she'd been staring. She felt her cheeks heat up. "No, I just... I still can't believe I'm here. With you. It feels like a dream."

Yuri's expression softened. He reached out, cupping her cheek with his hand. "If it's a dream," he said softly, "then I don't ever want to wake up."

The air between them crackled with tension. Beth's eyes flicked to Yuri's lips, then back to his eyes. He was leaning in ever so slowly...

The taxi came to an abrupt stop, jerking them apart. "We're here," the driver announced in heavily accented English.

Beth let out a breath she hadn't realized she'd been holding. Yuri cleared his throat, looking both frustrated and amused.

"Perfect timing," he muttered, then louder, "Shall we, moye solnyshko?"

As they stepped out onto the snowy streets of Minsk, Beth gasped. The city was a winter wonderland, strings of lights twinkling in the early evening darkness.

"It's beautiful," she breathed.

"Yes, it is," Yuri agreed, but when Beth turned to look at him, he was staring at her, not the scenery.

He held out his hand. "Ready for your first taste of Belarus?"

Beth laced her fingers through his, marveling at how perfectly they fit together. "Ready as I'll ever be."

As Yuri led her into a cozy-looking restaurant, Beth felt a thrill of excitement. This was just the beginning of their adventure. And if the electricity she felt every time Yuri touched her was any indication, it was going to be one hell of a ride.

The restaurant was warm and inviting, filled with the aroma of hearty food and the soft murmur of conversation. Yuri guided Beth to a secluded corner table, his hand resting lightly on the small of her back. Even through her coat, his touch sent sparks along her skin.

"So," Yuri said as they settled into their seats, "what do you think of Minsk so far?"

Beth smiled, taking in the rustic decor and the twinkling lights strung across the ceiling. "It's magical- like stepping into a fairy tale."

"Just wait until you try the food," Yuri winked. He rattled off an order in rapid-fire Russian, the words rolling off his tongue in a way that made Beth's stomach do a little flip.

As they waited for their food, conversation flowed easily between them, punctuated by lingering glances and 'accidental' brushes of hands across the table. It was as if all those weeks of virtual communication had laid a foundation, and now they were building something real and tangible on top of it.

When the food arrived, Beth's eyes widened at the spread before them. "Wow," she breathed, "I hope you plan to help me eat all this."

Yuri's eyes twinkled mischievously. "Oh, I plan to help you with a lot of things during your stay, moye solnyshko."

Beth nearly choked on her kvass, the implications of his words sending a rush of heat through her body. Two could play that game.

She leaned forward, deliberately letting her foot brush against his leg under the table. "I'm counting on it, Mr. Minsk."

Yuri's eyes darkened, his Adam's apple bobbing as he swallowed hard. For a moment, the air between them was thick with unspoken desire.

Then Beth broke the tension with a laugh. "Now, are you going to teach me how to eat these potato pancakes properly, or do I have to figure it out myself?"

As the meal progressed, Beth found herself falling even harder for Yuri. His laugh, the way his eyes crinkled when he smiled, the gentle teasing in his voice – it was all so much more potent in person. And the way he looked at her... like she was the most fascinating thing he'd ever seen.

By the time they finished dessert – a decadent honey cake that Yuri insisted was "just like his babushka used to make" – Beth was feeling warm and slightly giddy, though whether from the food, the company, or the subtle flirting, she couldn't be sure.

As they stepped back out into the snowy night, Yuri took her hand again. "So, what next? Are you up for a little adventure, or would you prefer to rest?"

Beth squeezed his hand, feeling bold. "I'm up for anything, as long as it's with you."

Yuri's answering smile was brilliant. "In that case, I know just the place. Do you trust me?"

"Completely," Beth said, surprised to find she meant it wholeheartedly.

Yuri's expression softened. He brought her hand to his lips, pressing a gentle kiss to her knuckles. "Then let's go make some memories, moye solnyshko."

As they set off down the twinkling streets of Minsk, hand in hand, Beth felt a sense of anticipation building. Whatever Yuri had planned, she knew one thing for certain: this would be a night – and a trip – she'd never forget.

Nine

Y uri guided Beth through Minsk's winding streets. Their breaths mingled in the crisp air.

"So, are you going to tell me where we're going?" Beth asked, a hint of playful impatience in her voice.

Yuri's eyes twinkled mischievously. "Patience, moye solnyshko. We're almost there."

As they rounded a corner, Beth gasped. Before them stretched a vast outdoor ice rink, surrounded by twinkling lights and festive decorations. Couples glided across the ice, their laughter carrying on in the night air.

"Ice skating?" Beth said, a mix of excitement and trepidation in her voice. "You remembered."

Yuri squeezed her hand. "Of course. I remember everything you tell me." His voice dropped lower, sending a shiver down her spine that had nothing to do with the cold. "Including your need for, ah, mouth-to-mouth assistance."

Beth felt her cheeks warm despite the chill. "Well, let's hope it doesn't come to that. Though with my skating skills, you never know."

They rented skates and made their way to the ice. Beth wobbled as she took her first step, instinctively grabbing Yuri's arm. He steadied her, his hand warm on her waist.

"I've got you," he murmured, his lips close to her ear. "Just hold onto me."

Beth looked up at him, suddenly very aware of how close they were. "I plan to," she said softly.

For a moment, they just stood there, lost in each other's eyes. Then Yuri cleared his throat, a slight flush coloring his cheeks. "Shall we?"

They glided onto the ice, Beth clinging to Yuri's arm. At first, she was stiff with concentration, her eyes fixed on her feet. But gradually, with Yuri's gentle guidance and a constant stream of encouragement, she began to relax.

"See? You're a natural," Yuri said, his voice warm with pride.

Beth laughed, the sound bright in the cold air. "I think you might be a bit biased, Mr. Minsk. But I appreciate the compliment."

As they made their way around the rink, Beth became increasingly aware of every point of contact between them - Yuri's hand on her waist, her arm looped through his, the brush of their legs as they glided along. It was intoxicating.

Feeling bold, Beth attempted a little twirl. Unfortunately, her confidence outweighed her skill. She felt herself losing balance, arms windmilling comically.

"Yuri!" she yelped, bracing for impact with the ice.

But instead of cold hardness, she felt strong arms wrap around her, pulling her against a solid chest. She looked up to find Yuri's face inches from hers, his blue eyes wide with concern and something else... heat?

"Are you okay?" he asked, his breath warm on her face.

Beth nodded, suddenly breathless for reasons that had nothing to do with her near fall. "My hero," she managed to say, her voice barely above a whisper.

Yuri's gaze dropped to her lips, then back to her eyes. The world seemed to shrink to just the two of them, the sounds of the rink fading away. Slowly, almost imperceptibly, Yuri began to lean in.

Beth's heart raced. This was it. Their first kiss. She closed her eyes, tilting her face up to meet his...

"Watch out!"

A child's shout broke the moment. Beth's eyes flew open just in time to see a young boy careen into them, sending all three sprawling onto the ice in a tangle of limbs and startled yelps.

For a second, there was stunned silence. Then Beth started to giggle. The giggles quickly turned into full-blown laughter, and soon Yuri joined in, his deep chuckles harmonizing with her lighter tones.

"I'm so sorry!" the boy said, looking mortified.

Yuri waved off his apology, still chuckling as he helped Beth to her feet. "No harm done. Are you both alright?"

As the boy skated off, Beth turned to Yuri, suddenly shy. "So... that happened."

Yuri's eyes crinkled as he smiled, reaching out to brush a stray snowflake from her cheek. "Indeed, it did. Though I must say, I had imagined our first kiss going a bit differently."

Beth's breath caught. "Oh? You've imagined it, have you?"

Yuri's gaze intensified, his voice dropping low. "More times than I care to admit."

The air between them crackled with tension once again. Beth licked her lips, noticing how Yuri's eyes tracked the movement. "Maybe we should try again," she suggested, her voice barely above a whisper. "Somewhere with less... traffic."

Yuri's answering smile was slow and full of promise. "I know just the place."

They returned their skates and made their way out of the rink, hands intertwined. As they walked, Beth felt a delicious anticipation building. Every glance, every touch seemed charged with electricity.

Yuri led her to a small park nearby, the trees adorned with twinkling lights. They stopped beneath a large evergreen, its branches heavy with snow.

"Better?" Yuri asked, turning to face her. His eyes were dark, intense.

Beth nodded, not trusting her voice. Yuri stepped closer, one hand coming up to cup her cheek. His touch was warm against her cold skin.

"Beth," he murmured, his accent wrapping around her name like a caress. "May I kiss you?"

Instead of answering, Beth rose up on her tiptoes, closing the distance between them. Their lips met, soft and tentative at first, then with growing passion. Yuri's arm wrapped around her waist, pulling her flush against him as Beth's hands found their way into his hair.

The kiss was everything Beth had imagined and more. Yuri tasted of honey cake and promises of adventure and home all at once. When they finally parted, both slightly breathless, Beth felt as though her whole world had shifted on its axis.

Yuri rested his forehead against hers, his eyes closed. "Beth," he breathed.

Beth laughed softly. "Um, yeah. Wow."

Yuri opened his eyes, his gaze full of warmth and something that looked a lot like adoration. "You know," he said, a hint of mischief in his voice, "I think we might need more practice. Just to be sure we've got it right."

Beth grinned, her heart soaring. "Well, Mr. Minsk, I do believe in thorough research. Shall we conduct a few more experiments?"

Yuri's answering laugh was swallowed by another kiss, deeper and more heated than the first. Surrounded by falling snowflakes, Beth knew coming to Belarus was her best decision.

Ten

S unlight streamed through the curtains, filling Beth's hotel room with warmth. She stretched, recalling the events from the previous night. A smile spread across her face as she remembered Yuri's kisses, his warm embrace, and how he'd looked at her like she was the most precious thing in the world.

A knock at the door jolted her from her reverie. "Room service!" a cheerful voice called out.

Confused, Beth wrapped herself in a robe and padded to the door. As she opened it, she was greeted not by a hotel employee but by Yuri, who was holding a tray laden with breakfast foods and wearing a mischievous grin.

"Surprise," he said, his eyes twinkling. "I thought you might be hungry after all that, ah, 'cultural exchange' last night."

Beth felt her cheeks warm at the memory of their heated goodnight kisses. "You're incorrigible," she laughed, stepping aside to let him in. "But also, very sweet. Thank you."

Yuri set the tray down on the small table by the window, then turned to Beth, his expression softening. "Good morning, moye solnyshko," he murmured, pulling her into his arms.

As Beth eased into Yuri's arms, she tilted her head upwards, inviting him to kiss her. His lips met hers willingly, their warmth seeping into her skin. The initial soft peck of a good morning greeting quickly evolved into something more intense, rekindling the passionate blaze that had consumed them just hours ago in the darkness of the night.

Underneath her robe, a heat began to radiate from between her thighs, a sensual warmth that was both new and familiar. It was a silent testament to their shared desire. As Yuri pressed himself closer against her, she could feel his arousal through the thin fabric of her robe. It nestled snugly between the folds, fueling the fire within her.

When they eventually pulled away from each other, gasping slightly for air but unwilling to completely break contact, Yuri gently leaned his forehead against hers. "I could get used to this," he murmured softly into the space between them.

"Me too," Beth admitted, her heart fluttering. Then, trying to lighten the suddenly intense mood, she added, "But maybe we should eat before the food gets cold? I'm dying to try whatever smells so delicious."

Yuri chuckled, releasing her with obvious reluctance. "Of course. I brought you a true Belarusian breakfast. Prepare your taste buds for an adventure."

As they settled at the table, Beth couldn't help but marvel at how comfortable this felt. Here she was, in a foreign country with a man she'd only just met in person, and yet it felt like the most natural thing in the world.

"So," Yuri said as Beth bit into a blini topped with sour cream and caviar, "I was thinking we could visit the Christmas market today. It's quite famous, you know. Unless you'd prefer to see some of the historical sites?"

Beth swallowed her bite, considering. "The market sounds wonderful. Although..." she trailed off, suddenly remembering something.

"Although?" Yuri prompted, raising an eyebrow.

Beth bit her lip. "Well, it's just... I may have promised my friends I'd scope out the competition. For the bakery, I mean."

Yuri's eyes lit up with interest. "Ah yes, the famous Sweet Dreams. I'd almost forgotten I was in the presence of a master baker. Tell me, what sort of 'competition' are we talking about?"

And so, Beth found herself explaining the upcoming Christmas Baking Spectacular, her words punctuated by bites of the delicious breakfast. Yuri listened intently, asking questions and offering suggestions.

"You know," he said thoughtfully as Beth finished her explanation, "I might be able to help with that. The Christmas market has some of the best bakers in Belarus. It would be the perfect place to gather ideas."

Beth's eyes widened. "Really? That would be amazing! Are you sure you don't mind?"

Yuri reached across the table, taking her hand in his. "Beth, I want to know everything about your life, your passions. If that means spending a day taste-testing Christmas treats, well," he grinned, "I suppose I'll just have to make that sacrifice."

Beth laughed, squeezing his hand. "My hero," she teased. Then, more seriously, "Thank you, Yuri. For everything. This trip... it's already more than I could have imagined."

Yuri's expression softened. He brought her hand to his lips, pressing a gentle kiss to her knuckles. "It's my pleasure, moye solnyshko. Now, finish your breakfast. We have a busy day of espionage and pastry sampling ahead of us."

An hour later, they were strolling hand in hand through the bustling Christmas market. The air was filled with the scent of spiced wine and fresh-baked goods, colorful stalls lining the streets as far as the eye could see.

"Oh, Yuri," Beth breathed, taking it all in. "It's magical."

Yuri squeezed her hand, his eyes crinkling as he smiled down at her. "Just wait until you taste the food. Come, I know just where to start."

He led her to a stall manned by a jolly-looking woman with rosy cheeks. A sign proclaimed "Babushka's Best Bakery" in both Russian and English.

"Ah, Yuri!" the woman exclaimed. "It's been too long! And who is this lovely young lady?"

"Privet, Anya," Yuri greeted her warmly. "This is Beth. She's visiting from America and happens to be an excellent baker herself."

Beth felt herself blush at the compliment. "It's nice to meet you," she said, suddenly shy.

Anya's eyes twinkled. "An American baker! How delightful. You must try my pryaniki. They're an old family recipe."

As Anya bustled about, preparing a sampler plate, Yuri leaned down to whisper in Beth's ear. "Anya makes the best Christmas cookies in all of Belarus. If anyone can give you ideas for your competition, it's her."

Beth nodded, touched by Yuri's thoughtfulness. Beth's professional interest was piqued when Anya returned with a plate piled high with intricately decorated cookies.

She bit into one, and her eyes widened. "Oh, my goodness," she mumbled around the mouthful. "These are incredible."

Anya beamed. "You're too kind. Now, tell me about your bakery in America. What sort of treats do you make?"

As Beth launched into a description of Sweet Dreams, she felt Yuri's arm slip around her waist. He listened intently, occasionally chiming in with a comment or question. Beth was struck by how genuinely interested he seemed in her work.

They spent the next few hours exploring the market, sampling treats from various stalls, and chatting with the bakers. Yuri seemed to know everyone, effortlessly translating and making introductions.

By early afternoon, Beth's head was spinning with new ideas, and her stomach was pleasantly full. They found a quiet corner near a roaring fire pit, settling onto a bench with steaming cups of mulled wine.

"So," Yuri said, his arm draped casually over her shoulders, "do you think you've gathered enough intel for your baking spectacular?"

Beth nodded, leaning into him. "Definitely. I can't wait to try out some of these techniques when I get home. Thank you for this, Yuri. It's been amazing."

Yuri pressed a kiss to her temple. "I'm glad. Although," he added, a hint of sadness creeping into his voice, "I have to admit, I'm not looking forward to you leaving."

Beth felt her heart clench. She'd been trying not to think about the end of her trip, about having to say goodbye to Yuri. "Me neither," she admitted softly.

They sat in contemplative silence for a moment, the reality of their situation settling over them like a heavy blanket. Then Yuri straightened up with a determined look in his eye.

"Well then," he said, his voice full of forced cheer, "I suppose we'll just have to make the most of the time we have left. What do you say we head back to the hotel, warm up a bit, and then I'll take you out for a proper Belarusian dinner?"

Beth smiled, pushing aside her melancholy thoughts. "That sounds perfect."

As they made their way back through the market, hand in hand, Beth found herself stealing glances at Yuri. She wondered what would happen after she left. *Would she feel the same way? Would he?*

For now, she decided, she'd focus on enjoying every moment with Yuri. The future, with all its complications and uncertainties, could wait. After all, they still had a few days left of their Belarusian Christmas adventure.

And she intended to make every second count.

Eleven

♥

The hotel room was illuminated by the gentle flicker of candle-light, creating a dance of shadows on the walls. Beth stood by the window, watching snowflakes in the streetlights below. Behind her, she heard the pop of a champagne cork.

"To unexpected adventures," Yuri's voice was low and warm as he handed her a flute of bubbling champagne.

Beth turned, her breath catching at the sight of him. Yuri had changed for dinner, trading his casual day wear for a crisp white shirt and dark slacks. The top buttons of his shirt were undone, offering a tantalizing glimpse of his collarbone.

"And to new beginnings," Beth added, clinking her glass against his. Their eyes locked over the rims as they sipped, the air between them charged with unspoken desire.

Yuri set his glass down, stepping closer. His fingers traced the curve of her cheek, feather-light. "You look beautiful, moye solnyshko," he murmured.

Beth leaned into his touch, her skin tingling. "You're not so bad yourself, Mr. Minsk."

His answering smile was slow and full of promise. He leaned in, his lips brushing against her ear as he whispered, "Perhaps we should skip dinner."

A shiver ran down Beth's spine. She pulled back slightly, meeting his heated gaze. "But you promised me a proper Belarusian meal," she teased, her voice breathier than intended.

Yuri's eyes darkened. "I did, didn't I? Well, I suppose I'll just have to make it worth the wait."

Before Beth could formulate a response, Yuri's lips met hers. It was an intoxicating mix of sweet and spicy. Her body softened against his, her senses surrendering to the raw heat radiating from him.

Her fingers traced a slow, deliberate path up his chest, each button of his shirt feeling like a heated stone beneath her touch. The firmness of his pectoral muscles under her hands sent shivers down her spine, making her heartbeat faster and louder in her ears.

Tangling her fingers into his thick hair felt like dipping them into warm silk. She tugged gently at the strands, eliciting a low groan from deep within Yuri's throat. It was raw and primal and echoed in every corner of the room.

Yuri's arms coiled around her waist like iron bands, pulling her closer until there was no space left between them. His grip tightened as if he feared she might slip away, anchoring her to him. The warmth of his body seeped through their clothes, enveloping them both in an intimate cocoon.

When they finally parted, both slightly breathless, Yuri rested his forehead against hers. "We should go," he said, though he made no move to release her. "Our reservation..."

"Right," Beth nodded, equally reluctant to break their embrace. "Dinner. We should definitely go to dinner."

Another moment passed before they finally stepped apart. Yuri offered his arm with an exaggerated bow. "Shall we, my lady?"

Beth laughed, linking her arm through his. "Lead the way, good sir."

The restaurant Yuri had chosen was intimate and cozy, with exposed brick walls and candlelit tables. As they were led to their seats, Beth noticed several patrons eyeing Yuri appreciatively. She felt a surge of possessiveness, pressing closer to his side.

Yuri, seemingly oblivious to the attention, pulled out Beth's chair for her. As she sat, he leaned down, his lips brushing her ear. "You know, your jealous face is incredibly sexy."

Beth felt her cheeks warm. "I don't know what you're talking about," she muttered, hiding behind her menu.

Yuri chuckled, taking his own seat. "Of course not. Now, shall I order for us? I promise to introduce you to the best Belarus has to offer."

As Yuri conversed with the waiter in rapid-fire Russian, Beth found herself captivated by how his lips formed the unfamiliar words, the subtle shifts of his expressions. When he turned back to her, catching her staring, his smile was knowing.

"See something you like?" he asked, his voice low and teasing.

Beth took a sip of her wine, gathering her courage. "Maybe," she replied, holding his gaze. "I'm still... sampling the menu."

Yuri's eyes darkened at her words. He reached across the table, his fingers intertwining with hers. "Well then," he said, his thumb tracing circles on her palm, "I hope you find something... satisfying."

The rest of the meal passed in a haze of delicious food and charged glances. Every accidental brush of hands, every shared smile, felt like foreplay. By the time dessert arrived – a decadent chocolate cake that Yuri insisted was "just like his babushka used to make" – Beth was practically squirming in her seat.

As Yuri fed her a bite of cake from his fork, his eyes never leaving hers, Beth made a decision. It was time to seize the moment.

"Yuri," she said, her voice husky, "take me back to the hotel."

His eyes widened slightly, then darkened with understanding. Without a word, he signaled for the check.

The taxi ride back to the hotel was torturous. They sat close, Yuri's hand resting on her thigh, his thumb tracing maddening circles on the fabric of her dress. Beth's entire body thrummed with anticipation.

The moment the elevator doors clanged shut, Yuri wasted no time. With a predatory swiftness, he had her pinned against the cold steel wall, his lips searing a fervent path to hers. His kiss was like wildfire, igniting a blaze that consumed them both.

Beth met his passion with equal fervor, her fingers clawing at the fabric of his shirt. She balled it in her fists, pulling him closer as she sought to lose herself in the intoxicating taste of him.

A low growl escaped from Yuri's throat as Beth's hand daringly ventured lower. Her fingers found evidence of his arousal straining against the confines of his trousers. A gasp slipped past her lips and into their shared breaths when she felt the hard outline of him.

"Yuri," she breathed out huskily against his mouth, her voice laced with desire. "I need you."

His response was a guttural groan that vibrated through her body like an electric current. "Beth," he rasped back, hot breath fanning over her neck as he nipped at her sensitive skin. "You're driving me crazy."

As the elevator doors opened, they stumbled out onto their floor, giggling and shushing each other like teenagers. At the door to Beth's room, Yuri paused, his expression suddenly serious.

"Beth," he said softly, cupping her face in his hands.

Beth silenced him with a kiss, her tongue darting into his mouth with urgent need. "I want you so much," she breathed against his lips. "I need this. Now."

Yuri's grin was pure sin, a promise of the pleasure to come. He opened the door and in one swift motion, swept Beth off her feet, her surprised gasp morphing into a moan as he pressed her against his hard body. He kicked the door shut and strode to the bed, his intent clear in his heated gaze.

He dropped her onto the plush bedspread, his muscular body rippling under his shirt as he crawled over her, a predator ready to devour its prey. His eyes roamed over her body, filled with a hunger that made her heart pound and her body ache. This was more than just lust; it was a primal, consuming need.

His lips crashed onto hers, their tongues clashing in a wild dance. His hands were everywhere, rough and demanding as they explored her body. He squeezed her breasts, pinched her nipples, and she arched into him, a gasp tearing from her throat.

Yuri growled, a low, feral sound, as he trailed hot, wet kisses down her neck, his mouth latching onto her nipple, sucking hard before biting gently. Beth cried out, her body writhing under his touch. He moved lower, his hands gripping her thighs, spreading them wide as he settled between them.

Through his pants, his cock was a hard, throbbing line against her thigh. She reached for it, stroking its length before unbuttoning his pants and shoving them down. He sprang free, thick and hard, the tip glistening with pre-cum. She wrapped her hand around him, stroking firmly, and he thrust into her touch with a groan.

"Fuck, you're perfect," Yuri grunted, his eyes wild as he took in her body, bare and ready for him.

He shifted lower, his tongue darting out to taste her, licking her clit with firm, steady strokes. Her body jerked, her hips bucking as he brought her to the edge, her orgasm crashing over her in a wave of pleasure.

Beth reached for him, her body still trembling, and pulled him up. She pushed him onto his back and straddled him, her wet pussy sliding against his cock. He gripped her hips, trying to guide her onto him, but she resisted, teasing him with a wicked grin.

"Fuck, Beth," he growled, his body taut with need.

She leaned down, her breath hot on his ear. "How bad do you want it?" she whispered, her voice sultry and low.

With a snarl, he flipped her onto her back, his body covering hers. "I. Fucking. Need. You," he grunted, each word punctuated by a thrust of his cock against her wet entrance.

He slammed into her, filling her completely. Their bodies moved together, a fierce, carnal rhythm that left them both panting and moaning. His cock pounded into her, hard and deep, each thrust sending waves of pleasure coursing through her body.

He flipped her onto her hands and knees, his fingers digging into her hips as he fucked her from behind, his thrusts wild and uncontrolled. Their bodies slapped together, the sound of their fucking filling the room, mingling with their gasps and moans.

Beth pushed back against him, meeting each thrust with a wild abandon that matched his own. She screamed his name as she came, her body convulsing around his cock. With a roar, he followed her over the edge, his cock pulsing as he filled her with his hot release.

Panting heavily in the aftermath of their shared climax, Beth looked into his eyes. Wild, hungry, and completely consumed by their passion, she knew this was just the beginning.

Twelve

♥

Golden streaks appeared on the tangled sheets as the morning sunlight filtered through. Beth stirred, her eyes fluttering open to find Yuri's intense blue gaze fixed on her. A slow smile spread across her face as memories of the night before flooded her senses.

"See something you like?" she murmured, her voice husky with sleep.

Yuri's lips curved into a devilish grin. "Mmm, I'd say it's more than just 'like." His fingers traced a lazy path down her bare arm, leaving goosebumps in their wake. "How did you sleep, moye solnyshko?"

Beth stretched languidly, enjoying the way Yuri's eyes darkened as the sheet slipped lower. "Like a dream. Though I'm not entirely convinced I'm awake yet."

"No?" Yuri's eyebrow quirked playfully. "Perhaps I should pinch you, just to be sure."

Beth giggled, swatting his hand away as it inched towards her ribs. "Don't you dare! I have other ideas for those hands of yours."

"Oh?" Yuri leaned in closer, his breath warm against her ear. "Do tell, Ms. Mason. I'm all ears... among other things."

A shiver ran down Beth's spine at his suggestive tone. She opened her mouth to respond but was cut off by a loud grumble from her stomach. Heat flooded her cheeks as Yuri burst into laughter.

"Perhaps we should feed you first," he chuckled, kissing her forehead before rolling out of bed. Beth couldn't help but admire the view as he stretched, all lean muscle and tanned skin.

"Like what you see?" Yuri teased, catching her stare.

Beth grinned unabashedly. "Just admiring the local scenery. It's quite... impressive."

Beth's answering laugh was rich and warm. He tossed her one of the hotel's fluffy robes. "Come on, you vixen. Let's get some food in you before you decide to consume me whole."

Beth slipped on the robe, allowing it to gape open slightly, revealing a hint of her curves as she followed him to the small kitchenette. "Don't tempt me," she purred, her eyes lingering on his body.

Beth stood behind the counter as Yuri busied himself with the coffee maker. "So, what's on the agenda for today?" she asked, her voice laced with suggestion. "More sightseeing? Or perhaps... something more intimate?"

Yuri turned, coffee pot in hand, his eyes smoldering with desire. "Well, I was thinking we could start with a thorough exploration of this room," he said, setting down the pot and stepping between her legs, his hands sliding up her thighs. "After all, we've hardly begun to plumb the depths of its... possibilities."

Beth's pulse quickened, her breath hitching as his fingers brushed against her intimate heat. "And what kind of possibilities did you have in mind, Mr. Minsk?" she asked, her voice barely a whisper.

Yuri leaned in closer, his breath hot on her ear. "Why don't I show you instead?" he murmured, his lips grazing her neck. His hand cupped her breast, his thumb circling her nipple through the thin fabric of the robe.

Their coffee cups sat forgotten as Yuri claimed Beth's lips with a fierce, demanding kiss that left her gasping for breath. She wrapped her legs around his waist, pulling him closer as his hands explored her body, untying her robe and letting it fall open.

Yuri's mouth moved from her lips to her neck, then lower, his tongue trailing a path of fire down to her breasts. He took one nipple into his mouth, sucking and biting gently as Beth arched her back, moaning with pleasure.

He continued his exploration, kissing every inch of her skin as if it were sacred ground. Beth shivered with anticipation as he moved lower, his hands gripping her thighs and spreading them wide. He knelt before her, his tongue delving into her most intimate place, licking and sucking until she was writhing against him, her hands fisted in his hair.

"Oh God, Yuri..." she gasped, her body convulsing as waves of pleasure washed over her. He stood up, his eyes never leaving hers as he untied his own robe, revealing his hard, ready length.

He lifted her onto the kitchen counter, positioning himself at her entrance. With one swift thrust, he buried himself deep inside her. Beth cried out, her nails digging into his back as he filled her completely.

Their moans filled the room as Yuri moved inside her with powerful, rhythmic thrusts. The counter creaked beneath them, the sound echoing the primal rhythm of their lovemaking. Beth met each thrust with her own, her hips rising to meet his, their bodies slick with sweat.

"You feel so good," Yuri groaned, his fingers finding her clit and circling it in time with his thrusts. Beth's body tensed, her inner muscles clenching around him as another orgasm ripped through her.

Yuri thrust harder, faster, his control shattering as Beth's climax pushed him over the edge. He came with a roar, his body shaking with the force of his release. They clung to each other, panting heavily as they rode out the waves of pleasure together before finally collapsing against each other, their bodies entwined on the kitchen counter.

Later, much later in the afternoon, they finally emerged from the hotel room, disheveled but glowing. The streets of Minsk were alive with pre-Christmas bustle, the air crisp and filled with the scent of mulled wine and fresh pastries.

"I can't believe I only have two days left," Beth sighed, leaning into Yuri's side as they strolled through a picturesque park. Snow-laden branches glittered in the afternoon sun, creating a winter wonderland around them.

Yuri's arm tightened around her waist. "Then we'll just have to make them count, won't we?" His eyes twinkled as he suddenly spun her around, pulling her into an impromptu dance.

Beth laughed, delighted, as he twirled her beneath the snowy boughs. "Yuri! What are you doing?"

"Dancing with the most beautiful woman in Belarus," he replied smoothly, dipping her low. "Is that a crime?"

As he pulled her back up, Beth cupped his face in her hands, kissing him deeply. She poured all the emotions she couldn't yet voice into that kiss – the joy, the wonder, the growing love she felt for this man who had swept into her life like a whirlwind.

When they parted, both slightly breathless, Yuri's eyes were shining with an emotion that mirrored her own. For a moment, they just stood there, lost in each other's gaze, oblivious to the curious glances of passersby.

Finally, Beth broke the silence. "So, Mr. Minsk," she said, her voice husky, "are there any more hidden talents you'd like to demonstrate?"

Yuri's answering grin was positively wicked. "Oh, moye solnyshko, you have no idea. But I'd be happy to give you a private showing."

Beth felt heat pool in her belly at his words. "Well then," she said, tugging him towards the park exit, "what are we waiting for?"

As they hurried back to the hotel, laughing and stealing kisses along the way, Beth marveled at how right this felt.

Thirteen

♥

T he familiar scent of vanilla and cinnamon enveloped Beth as she pushed open the doors of Sweet Dreams. Home. After her whirlwind week in Belarus, the cozy bakery felt both comforting and slightly surreal.

"She lives!" Reese's voice rang out from behind the counter. "I was starting to think you'd decided to defect to the land of vodka and fur hats."

Beth rolled her eyes, dropping her bags and enveloping her assistant in a tight hug. "Missed you too, smartass. How's everything been?"

Reese's eyes twinkled mischievously. "Oh, you know, same old, same old. Although..." she leaned in conspiratorially, "Zack's been in here every day asking about you. I think someone's got a crush."

Beth felt a pang of guilt. In all the excitement with Yuri, she'd completely forgotten about Zack's attempts at flirting. "Reese, I—"

"Relax, boss," Reese cut her off with a knowing smirk. "I've seen that look before. How was the trip?"

Before Beth could respond, the bell above the door chimed. Jessie burst in, her cheeks flushed from the cold.

"Beth! You're back!" she exclaimed, pulling her friend into an enthusiastic hug. "How was Belarus? Did you find any scientific advancements in pastry technology? Oh! Did you bring back any samples for analysis?"

Beth laughed, extricating herself from Jessie's grip. "Slow down, Jess. I've barely had time to put my bags down."

"Right, sorry," Jessie said, not looking sorry at all. "It's just that the Christmas Baking Spectacular is in three days. I've been working on some theories about optimal sugar crystallization that I think could really give us an edge."

"Three days?" Beth felt her stomach drop. How had she lost track of time so completely?

Reese raised an eyebrow. "Please tell me you didn't forget about the competition you've obsessed over for weeks."

"Of course not," Beth lied, her mind racing. "I just... lost track of the days a bit. But don't worry, I've got plenty of ideas from Belarus. We're going to blow this competition out of the water."

As if on cue, her phone buzzed. Beth's heart skipped a beat as she saw Yuri's name on the screen.

Yuri: *Missing you already, moye solnyshko. How was your flight?*

Beth bit her lip, trying to suppress a grin as she typed back:

Beth: *Landed safely but experiencing severe Yuri withdrawal. Might need to book a return trip ASAP.*

"Earth to Beth," Reese's voice cut through her Yuri-induced haze. "Care to share with the class?"

Beth looked up to find Reese and Jessie watching her with matching expressions of curiosity. She sighed, knowing there was no point in trying to hide her happiness.

"Yuri is amazing," she admitted. "My trip to see him and his country was amazing."

Reese's eyes widened. "I'm so glad. I still can't believe you went to see a man you only have known online for a few weeks. Beth Mason, you dark horse! I didn't think you had it in you."

Beth protested weakly. "We just... connected. And now..."

"You've been googly-eyed and giggly for weeks," Reese finished for her. "It's disgustingly cute. I approve."

Jessie, who had been uncharacteristically quiet, suddenly piped up. "Now that you've spent time with him, have you considered the logistical challenges? The time difference alone would require significant schedule adjustments, not to mention the potential visa issues if things progressed—"

"Whoa, slow down there, Einstein," Reese laughed. "Let's let Beth enjoy the honeymoon phase before we start planning international relocations."

Beth's phone buzzed again. Another message from Yuri:

Yuri: *Funny you should mention that. How would you feel about having a very enthusiastic cheerleader at your baking competition?*

Beth's heart leaped. She quickly typed back:

Beth: *Are you serious? You'd come all this way?*

Yuri: *For you, moye solnyshko, I'd cross oceans. Plus, I hear there might be cookies involved. How could I resist?*

"Okay, that's it," Reese said, plucking the phone from Beth's hands. "No more lovey-dovey texting until you fill us in on everything. And I do mean everything."

For the next hour, as they prepped the bakery for opening, Beth regaled Reese and Jessie with tales of her Belarusian adventure. She told them about the Christmas markets, the delicious food, and, of course, Yuri. By the time she finished, Reese was sighing dramatically, and Jessie was scribbling notes about Belarusian baking techniques.

"So," Reese said as they put the finishing touches on a tray of croissants, "when do we get to meet this paragon of Belarusian manhood?"

Beth's phone chimed again. She read the message, a grin spreading across her face. "Sooner than you might think. He's coming for the competition."

Reese's jaw dropped. "Shut up! Seriously? Oh, this is going to be good."

"Indeed," Jessie nodded thoughtfully. "It will provide an excellent opportunity for cultural exchange and comparative analysis of baking methodologies."

Beth and Reese shared an amused look. "Right," Beth said. "That's definitely why he's coming. For the... baking methodologies."

The bell above the door chimed again. This time, it was Kelly, looking windswept and excited. "There's my globe-trotting girl!" she exclaimed, pulling Beth into a tight hug. "You, missy, have some explaining to do. I want every juicy detail."

As Beth opened her mouth to respond, the door chimed once more. Zack walked in, a hopeful smile on his face and a bag from The Daily Grind in his hand.

"Beth! You're back," he said, his eyes lighting up. "I, uh, brought you some of that new blend we were working on. Thought it might help with the jet lag."

Beth felt a twinge of guilt at the eagerness in his voice. "Thanks, Zack. That's really thoughtful of you."

An awkward silence fell over the bakery. Reese, ever the peacekeeper, clapped her hands together. "Right! Well, as fun as this reunion is, we've got a baking competition to prepare for. Zack, why don't you tell Beth about those coffee-infused scones you were working on?"

As Zack launched into an enthusiastic description of his latest creation, Beth's mind wandered. In just three days, she'd compete in the biggest baking event of her career. And Yuri would be there, watching. The thought sent a mix of excitement and nerves fluttering through her stomach.

Her phone buzzed again. Another message from Yuri:

Yuri: *Ticket booked. I'll be there in two days. Try not to miss me too much until then.*

Beth couldn't suppress her smile as she typed back:

Beth: *Too late. Already missing you. Can't wait to see you. And to introduce you to everyone.*

"Okay, lovebirds," Kelly's voice cut through her thoughts. "Enough texting. We've got work to do. Beth, honey, I love you, but you look like you've been hit by the happy stick. We need to get you focused."

Beth nodded, reluctantly putting her phone away. "You're right. Okay, team. Let's talk about strategy. This competition isn't going to win itself."

As they gathered around the central workstation, Beth felt a surge of determination. She had her friends, her bakery, and soon, she'd have Yuri by her side. The Christmas Baking Spectacular didn't stand a chance.

"Alright," she said, tying on her apron. "Let's show this town what Sweet Dreams is made of."

The next two days passed in a blur of flour, sugar, and frantic preparation. Beth barely had time to think, let alone worry about Yuri's impending arrival. But as she stood in the airport's arrivals area, her heart pounding, all her nerves came rushing back.

What if the spark they'd felt in Belarus didn't translate to her world? What if he took one look at her small-town life and decided it wasn't for him?

Her spiraling thoughts were interrupted by a familiar voice. "Moye solnyshko."

Beth turned, and there he was. Yuri looked slightly rumpled from the long flight but still devastatingly handsome, his blue eyes crinkling as he smiled at her.

Without a word, she threw herself into his arms. He caught her easily, lifting her off her feet as he kissed her deeply.

When they finally parted, both slightly breathless, Yuri rested his forehead against hers. "Hello," he murmured.

Beth laughed, feeling giddy. "Hello yourself. Welcome to America."

Fourteen

♥

The bell above Sweet Dreams' door chimed merrily as Beth and Yuri entered, a gust of cold air following them inside. The bakery was a hive of activity, with Reese and Jessie darting between workstations like sugar-fueled bees.

"Honey, I'm home!" Beth called out, unable to keep the grin off her face. "And I brought a special delivery from Belarus!"

Reese's head popped up from behind a tower of mixing bowls, her eyes widening as she caught sight of Yuri. "Well, well, well," she drawled, wiping her hands on her apron as she approached. "If it isn't the famous Yuri in the flesh. I was starting to think Beth had imagined you."

Yuri chuckled, extending his hand. "Very much real, I assure you. And you must be Reese. Beth's told me so much about you."

"All lies, I'm sure," Reese winked, shaking his hand. "Though I must say, her descriptions didn't do you justice. No wonder she came back from Belarus with stars in her eyes."

"Reese!" Beth hissed, feeling her cheeks warm.

"What? I'm just stating facts," Reese said innocently. "Now, are you two lovebirds going to stand there all day, or are you going to help us prep for this competition?"

Before either could respond, Jessie emerged from the back room, her arms full of what looked suspiciously like scientific equipment. "Beth! Oh good, you're back. I've been running some experiments on sugar crystallization rates, and I think I've found a way to— oh!" She stopped short, noticing Yuri. "Hello. You must be the former premier nightclub owner. I'm Dr. Jessica Brooke, but you can call me Jessie. Everyone does."

Yuri raised an eyebrow at Beth, amusement dancing in his eyes. "Doctor? I didn't realize we'd have a scientist on our team."

"Oh, I'm not really on the team," Jessie explained earnestly. "I'm just here to provide empirical data and analysis to optimize Beth's recipes for maximum flavor impact and textural appeal."

"In other words," Reese translated, "she's our secret weapon. Speaking of which, we should probably get back to work. The competition's tomorrow, and we still have a ton to do."

Beth nodded, slipping off her coat. "Right. Yuri, I hope you don't mind jumping right in. We could really use an extra pair of hands."

Yuri's grin was positively wicked as he rolled up his sleeves. "Moye solnyshko, my hands are yours to command. Where do you want me?"

Reese let out a low whistle. "Oh, I like him. Can we keep him?"

"Down, girl," Beth laughed, tossing Yuri an apron. "Alright, team. Let's show this town what international collaboration looks like."

For the next few hours, the bakery was a whirlwind of activity. Beth and Yuri moved around each other with an effortless synchronicity, as if they'd been baking together for years instead of hours. Reese watched them with a knowing smirk, while Jessie flitted between workstations, muttering about molecular gastronomy and flavor profiles.

"So, Yuri," Reese said as she piped delicate rosettes onto a tray of cupcakes, "tell us more about this nightclub of yours. Beth mentioned it was quite the hotspot."

Yuri's smile dimmed slightly. "Ah, Rhapsody. It was... special. Imagine the energy of a thousand people, all moving as one to the beat. The lights, the music, the atmosphere – it was magic."

"Was?" Jessie asked, looking up from her refractometer. "Did something happen?"

A heavy silence fell over the kitchen. Beth reached out, gently squeezing Yuri's hand. He gave her a grateful smile before turning back to Reese and Jessie.

"There was a fire," he explained quietly. "We lost everything. Incl uding... including a dear friend."

"Oh, Yuri," Reese breathed. "I'm so sorry. That must have been awful."

Yuri nodded; his eyes distant. "It was. For a while, I thought I'd never find that kind of passion again. But then..." his gaze shifted to Beth, softening, "I found a new kind of magic."

"Aww," Reese cooed. "That's disgustingly sweet. I love it."

"Indeed," Jessie nodded seriously. "The parallels between nightclub management and bakery operations are quite fascinating. Both require a keen understanding of crowd dynamics, sensory stimulation, and product delivery. Perhaps we could design a series of experiments to—"

"Or," Reese cut in, "we could focus on not burning these cupcakes. Jess, can you check the oven?"

As Jessie hurried to rescue the cupcakes, the bell above the door chimed again. This time, it was Kelly who burst in, her arms laden with shopping bags.

"Alright, my little sugar plums," she announced, "Mama's here with reinforcements. I've got energy drinks, snacks, and— well, hello there, tall, dark, and handsome!"

Yuri chuckled, extending his hand. "You must be the famous Kelly. I'm Yuri. It's a pleasure to finally meet you."

Kelly's eyes widened as she shook his hand. "My, my, Beth. You weren't exaggerating. The accent, the smile... if you ever need a taste tester for this particular dish, you just let me know."

"Kelly!" Beth exclaimed, torn between embarrassment and laughter.

"What? I'm just appreciating the view," Kelly winked. "Now, tell me everything. How's the prep going? Are we ready to crush this competition or what?"

As Beth filled Kelly in on their progress, Yuri found himself drawn into a debate with Jessie about the merits of various leavening agents. Reese watched it all with an amused smirk, shaking her head as she continued to decorate.

"I hate to break up this little United Nations of baking," she said eventually, "but we've got about twelve hours until showtime, and there's still a lot to do."

Beth nodded, clapping her hands together. "Right. Okay, team. Let's break this down. Reese, you focus on the decorations. Jessie, keep working on that sugar experiment, but maybe dial back the scientific jargon a notch. Kelly, you're on supply-run duty. Anything we need, you're our go-to girl. And Yuri..."

She trailed off, suddenly realizing she hadn't actually discussed with him how involved he wanted to be. "Yuri, you don't have to—"

"I'm all yours, moye solnyshko," he cut in, his eyes twinkling. "Just point me where you need me."

Beth felt a rush of affection. "In that case, you're with me. We've got a secret weapon to prepare."

As they all sprang into action, the bakery humming with renewed energy, Beth couldn't help but marvel at how perfectly Yuri fit into her world. It was as if he'd always been there, filling a space she hadn't even realized was empty.

Hours ticked by in a blur of flour, sugar, and increasingly punchy banter. As the sky outside began to lighten, signaling the approach of dawn, Beth called for a break.

"Alright, everyone," she said, stifling a yawn. "Power nap time. Twenty minutes, then we're back at it."

As the others settled onto various surfaces – Reese curling up in a chair, Jessie sprawling across a clear countertop, Kelly disappearing into the office – Beth found herself alone with Yuri for the first time in hours.

"Hey," she said softly, leaning into him. "How are you holding up?"

Yuri wrapped an arm around her, pressing a kiss to her temple. "I'm perfect. This... all of this... it's amazing, Beth. You're amazing."

Beth felt her heart swell. "I'm so glad you're here," she murmured. "I don't think I could do this without you."

Yuri tightened his embrace. "You could. You're stronger than you know. But I'm honored to be by your side."

They stood in comfortable silence for a moment, swaying slightly. Then Yuri spoke again, his voice hesitant. "Beth... what happens after the competition?"

Beth pulled back slightly, looking up at him. "What do you mean?"

Yuri ran a hand through his hair, a nervous gesture she was coming to recognize. "I mean... I fly back to Belarus in three days. And then what? I can't stop thinking about it. About you. About us."

Beth felt her breath catch. "Yuri..."

"I know it's crazy," he rushed on. "We've only known each other for a short time. But Beth, I've never felt this way before. The thought of going back, of not seeing you every day... it's killing me."

Beth's heart raced. She knew exactly how he felt because she felt the same way. The idea of him leaving was like a physical ache in her chest.

"So don't go," she whispered.

Yuri's eyes widened. "What?"

Beth took a deep breath, gathering her courage. "Don't go. Or... or if you have to go, come back. We can figure it out. Visas, work permits, whatever it takes. I just... I don't want to lose this. Lose you."

For a moment, Yuri just stared at her, his expression unreadable. Then, slowly, a smile spread across his face. "Moye solnyshko," he murmured, cupping her face in his hands. "My Beth. Are you asking me to move to America?"

Beth nodded, feeling simultaneously terrified and exhilarated. "I guess I am. Is that completely insane?"

Yuri's answering laugh was joyous. "Probably," he said, leaning in close. "But then, the best recipes often require a little madness, no?"

As their lips met in a deep, passionate kiss, Beth felt like her heart might burst with happiness. They still had a lot to figure out – the competition, the logistics of an international move, the future of their relationship – but in that moment, none of it mattered.

The sound of slow clapping broke them apart. They turned to find Reese, Jessie, and Kelly watching them with varying expressions of amusement and approval.

"Well," Reese drawled, "I guess that answers the question of whether Yuri's sticking around."

"Fascinating," Jessie mumbled, scribbling in her ever-present notebook. "The release of oxytocin and dopamine during moments of romantic connection can lead to heightened decision-making capabilities and increased risk tolerance. This could potentially impact Beth's performance in the competition. We should run some tests—"

"Or," Kelly cut in, "we could let the lovebirds have their moment and get back to prepping for this competition. After all," she added with a wink, "we've got a wedding cake to practice for now, don't we?"

Beth buried her face in Yuri's chest, laughing as her friends dissolved into excited chatter about international romances and fusion wedding menus. "Welcome to my world," she mumbled.

Yuri's chuckle rumbled through her. "It's perfect," he said softly. "You're perfect."

And as they turned back to the controlled chaos of competition prep, Beth couldn't help but agree. This – the bakery, her friends, Yuri by her side – was exactly where she was meant to be.

The Christmas Baking Spectacular didn't stand a chance.

Fifteen

The community center bustled with activity as contestants and spectators alike filed in for the Christmas Baking Spectacular. The air was thick with the scent of sugar and spice, punctuated by the occasional whir of a stand mixer or clang of a baking sheet.

Beth stood at her assigned station, surveying her ingredients with a critical eye. Yuri hovered nearby, ready to assist but careful not to overstep the competition rules.

"Nervous?" he asked, his voice low and soothing.

Beth took a deep breath, squaring her shoulders. "Terrified. Excited. A little nauseous. Is it possible to be all three at once?"

Yuri chuckled, discreetly squeezing her hand. "Perfectly normal, moye solnyshko. You've got this. Your macarons alone could bring world peace."

"Flattery will get you everywhere, Mr. Minsk," Beth grinned, some of the tension easing from her shoulders.

"Alright, lovebirds," Reese's voice cut in as she approached, arms laden with last-minute supplies. "Save the sweet talk for after we crush this competition."

Jessie trailed behind her, looking slightly frazzled. "I've calibrated all the measuring tools to ensure maximum accuracy," she reported. "And

I've prepared a series of charts detailing optimal baking temperatures and times based on relative humidity and barometric pressure."

Beth blinked. "That's... very thorough, Jess. Thanks."

"Oh, and I've also calculated the statistical probability of various flavor combinations appealing to the judges based on their publicly available dining preferences and social media activity," Jessie added, producing a thick binder from her bag.

Reese raised an eyebrow. "Jess, honey, I'm pretty sure that's cheating. And possibly stalking."

Before Jessie could protest, a booming voice echoed through the hall. "Ladies and gentlemen, welcome to the First Annual Stanford Christmas Baking Spectacular!"

Mayor Winters stood on a small stage, beaming at the crowd. "Today, we'll see the finest bakers in our lovely town compete for the coveted title of Stanford's Star Baker. Contestants, are you ready?"

A chorus of affirmatives rang out. Beth gripped her rolling pin tightly, adrenaline surging through her veins.

"Excellent!" Mayor Winters clapped her hands together. "You have four hours to create a showstopping Christmas dessert that captures the spirit of the season. On your mark... get set... BAKE!"

The hall erupted into a flurry of activity. Beth dove into action, her earlier nerves forgotten as she lost herself in the familiar rhythms of baking.

"Reese, can you start on the gingerbread while I tackle the macarons?" she called out, already reaching for the almond flour.

"On it, boss," Reese replied, expertly measuring molasses.

As Beth began piping perfect circles of macaron batter, she caught sight of Zack at a nearby station. He gave her a small wave, which she returned with a smile.

"Ah, is that the famous Zack?" Yuri asked, his tone light but with an undercurrent of... something. Jealousy?

Beth laughed, shaking her head. "Down, boy. Zack's just a friend. And speaking of friends, shouldn't you be cheering from the sidelines? Not that I don't appreciate the view, but I'm pretty sure having a personal assistant is against the rules."

Yuri held up his hands in mock surrender. "As you wish. But fir st..." He leaned in, pressing a quick kiss to her cheek. "For luck," he whispered before sauntering off to join Kelly in the spectator area.

"Girl," Reese said, her eyes wide, "if you don't marry that man, I will."

Beth felt her cheeks warm. "Let's focus on winning this competition first, shall we?"

The next few hours passed in a blur of flour, sugar, and increasingly complex baking techniques. Beth's vision for a winter wonderland dessert slowly took shape: a gingerbread castle surrounded by delicate snowflake macarons, with a mirror-glaze lake and spun-sugar icicles.

As she put the finishing touches on a fondant Santa, Beth became aware of a commotion at the far end of the hall.

"I'm telling you, it's not fair!" a shrill voice carried over the general hubbub. "She's got a whole team helping her!"

Beth looked up to see Gina, her former employee (and the reason for her breakup with Keith), gesturing wildly at Mayor Winters.

"Now, now," the Mayor said soothingly, "everyone's playing by the same rules here. Ms. Mason's assistants are registered contestants, just like your... er, helper."

Beth followed the Mayor's gaze to see Keith lurking behind Gina, looking distinctly uncomfortable.

"Oh boy," Reese muttered. "Drama at three o'clock."

"Ignore them," Beth said firmly, though her hands shook slightly as she piped a delicate border on her gingerbread castle. "We've got more important things to focus on."

But Gina wasn't done. She stormed over to Beth's station, her face flushed with anger. "You think you're so special, don't you? With your fancy bakery and your foreign boyfriend. Well, I've got news for you, Beth Mason. You're going down."

Beth straightened up, meeting Gina's glare head-on. "Gina, I'm sorry you feel that way. But this is a baking competition, not a personal vendetta. Why don't we let our desserts do the talking?"

"Oh, they'll talk alright," Gina sneered. "And when I win, everyone will see what a fraud you really are."

"Is there a problem here, ladies?" Yuri's voice, cool and collected, cut through the tension.

Gina's eyes widened as she took in Yuri's imposing figure. "N-no," she stammered. "No problem at all." She scurried back to her station, dragging a bewildered-looking Keith with her.

"You, okay?" Yuri asked softly, his hand a comforting presence on Beth's back.

Beth nodded, taking a deep breath. "I'm fine. Just... bringing back some not-so-great memories."

"Hey," Yuri said, gently turning her to face him. "You are talented, kind, and stronger than you know. Don't let anyone make you doubt that. Least of all them."

Beth felt a rush of affection for this man who had come to know her so well in such a short time. "Thank you," she murmured, resisting the urge to kiss him senselessly in front of the whole town.

"Anytime, moye solnyshko," Yuri winked. "Now, go show them what a real baker can do."

Reinvigorated, Beth threw herself back into her work. The final hour ticked by in a frenzy of last-minute adjustments and near disasters narrowly averted.

"Five minutes, bakers!" Mayor Winters called out.

Beth surveyed her creation with a critical eye. The gingerbread castle stood proud and tall, its spun-sugar windows glinting in the light. The macarons were perfectly formed, their ganache filling flavored with peppermint and cocoa. The mirror-glaze lake reflected the twinkling lights strung around the hall.

"It's beautiful, Beth," Reese breathed, admiring their handiwork.

"We did it," Beth said, a note of wonder in her voice. "We actually did it."

"Was there ever any doubt?" Jessie chimed in, still scribbling furiously in her notebook. "According to my calculations, the aesthetic appeal combined with the flavor profile gives us a 78.3% chance of victory."

Reese rolled her eyes fondly. "I'll take those odds."

"Time's up!" Mayor Winters announced. "Bakers, step away from your creations!"

As the judges made their rounds, sampling each dessert with serious expressions, Beth found herself gravitating towards Yuri. He wrapped an arm around her waist, pressing a kiss to her temple.

"Win or lose," he murmured, "I'm so proud of you."

Beth leaned into him, drawing strength from his steady presence. "Thank you for being here," she whispered. "For everything."

The judges conferred in hushed tones, their deliberations seeming to stretch on for an eternity. Finally, Mayor Winters stepped up to the microphone, a golden envelope in hand.

"Ladies and gentlemen, we have our winners! In third place... The Daily Grind Café, with their innovative coffee-infused Yule log!"

A smattering of applause filled the hall. Beth caught Zack's eye and gave him a thumbs up, which he returned with a gracious smile.

"In second place..." Mayor Winters paused dramatically, "Gina's Sweet Sensations, with their peppermint dream cake!"

Gina let out a shriek of delight, jumping up and down. Keith looked relieved, if a bit overwhelmed by her enthusiasm.

Beth's heart pounded in her chest. This was it. If they hadn't placed second, then...

"And the winner of the First Annual Stanford Christmas Baking Spectacular, and our town's official Star Baker, is..."

The room fell silent, the tension palpable.

"SWEET DREAMS BAKERY!"

The hall erupted into cheers. Beth stood frozen momentarily, unable to process what she'd just heard. Then Reese hugged her, Jessie rattled off statistics about their victory probability, and Yuri spun her around, his laughter mingling with hers.

"You did it, moye solnyshko!" he exclaimed, setting her down gently. "I knew you could."

As Mayor Winters presented her with an oversized check and a gaudy trophy, Beth felt as though she might burst with happiness. She'd done it. They'd done it. Sweet Dreams was officially Stanford's best bakery.

The celebration continued late into the night, with the entire town seeming to cram into Sweet Dreams for an impromptu victory party. As Beth moved through the crowd, accepting congratulations and fielding questions about her winning creation, she felt a tap on her shoulder.

She turned to find Zack holding two cups of coffee. "Congratulations," he said, offering her one of the cups. "You deserved it."

"Thanks, Zack," Beth smiled, genuinely touched by his graciousness. "Your Yule log was amazing. I loved the coffee twist."

Zack shrugged, a slight blush coloring his cheeks. "Well, I learned from the best. Listen, Beth, I... I'm happy for you. Truly. Yuri seems like a great guy."

Beth felt a rush of affection for her friend. "He is. And Zack? You're going to make someone very happy one day. You're a catch, you know."

Zack's blush deepened. "Yeah, well... maybe I just needed to open my eyes a bit. Speaking of which..." He glanced at Jessie, who animatedly explained something to a bemused-looking Kelly. "Do you think Jessie might want to grab coffee sometime? You know, to discuss the scientific aspects of baking?"

Beth grinned, patting his arm. "I think she'd love that. Go get 'em, tiger."

As Zack made his way over to Jessie, Beth felt arms encircle her waist from behind. "Having fun, Star Baker?" Yuri's voice rumbled in her ear.

Beth turned in his embrace, looping her arms around his neck. "The most fun. Although..." she bit her lip, suddenly feeling shy. "I can think of one way to make it even better."

Yuri's eyes darkened. "Oh? Do tell, moye solnyshko."

Instead of answering, Beth stretched up on her tiptoes, pressing her lips to his in a deep, passionate kiss. The noise of the party faded away, leaving just the two of them in their own little world.

When they finally parted, both slightly breathless, Beth rested her forehead against Yuri's. "Stay," she whispered. "Not just for a few more days. Stay for good."

Yuri's answering smile was radiant. "Beth Mason," he said softly, "I thought you'd never ask."

As they sealed their agreement with another kiss, oblivious to the knowing looks and good-natured teasing of their friends, Beth knew that this – right here, in Yuri's arms, surrounded by the people she loved in the bakery she'd built from the ground up – this was her true victory.

It was the best Christmas gift she could have ever had.

Sweet Dreams had won more than just a baking competition. It had won her a future filled with love, laughter, and endless possibilities.

And really, what could be sweeter than that?

The End

Coming Soon

♥

The Perfect Blend -Ladies of Stanford Book Two

T he cheerful tinkle of the bell above The Daily Grind's door barely registered over the post-competition buzz. Zack Harrington looked up from the espresso machine, his hands moving on autopilot as he crafted yet another latte. The café was packed, a sea of familiar faces riding the high of Stanford's first Christmas Baking Spectacular.

"One oat milk latte for Sarah," he called out, sliding the cup across the counter with a practiced smile. As Sarah reached for her drink, a flash of movement caught Zack's eye.

Dr. Jessica Brooke stumbled through the door; her arms laden with what looked suspiciously like scientific equipment. Her chestnut hair had escaped its usually neat bun, frizzing around her face like an Einstein-esque halo.

"Jessie?" Zack called out, raising an eyebrow. "Everything okay there?"

Jessie's head snapped up, her green eyes wide behind slightly askew glasses. "Zack! Yes, fine, absolutely tickety-boo. I just need to, um..." She glanced around wildly before making a beeline for an empty table in the corner.

Curiosity piqued, Zack signaled to his barista, Mike, to take over. He grabbed a towel, wiping his hands as he approached Jessie's table. She was already hunched over a notebook, scribbling furiously.

"Can I get you anything?" Zack asked, unable to keep the amusement from his voice. "Coffee? Tea? A particle accelerator, perhaps?"

Jessie looked up, blinking owlishly. "What? Oh, no, I'm fine. Unless..." Her eyes narrowed, focusing on Zack with sudden intensity. "Actually, do you have any of that Brazilian single-origin you were serving last week? The one with the hint of blackberry and dark chocolate notes?"

Zack's eyebrows shot up. "You remember that?"

A faint blush colored Jessie's cheek. "I have an eidetic memory. It's both a blessing and a curse. Did you know that the average human brain can store up to 2.5 petabytes of data? That's equivalent to about three million hours of TV shows. Of course, that's just a theoretical—"

"Jessie," Zack cut in gently, "the coffee?"

"Right! Yes, sorry. I'd love a cup, if you have it."

Zack nodded, a smile tugging at his lips. "Coming right up. And maybe you can explain what allthis is about?" He gestured to the equipment strewn across the table.

Jessie's eyes lit up. "Oh! Well, I was thinking about Beth's winning dessert from the competition. The gingerbread castle was structurally fascinating, but what really caught my attention was the mirror glaze on the lake. The molecular composition must be incredibly precise to achieve that level of reflectivity while maintaining optimal viscosity for pouring and setting. I hypothesized that by adjusting the ratio of gelatin to glucose syrup, we could potentially create a glaze with even greater tensile strength and light-refracting properties. Of course, that led me to consider the crystallization process of various sugar compounds under different atmospheric conditions, which is why I brought the hygrometer and..."

She trailed off, noticing Zack's blank stare. "And I'm boring you, aren't I? Sorry, I tend to get carried away."

Zack shook his head, chuckling. "Not boring, just... intense. Tell you what, let me get that coffee, and you can explain it to me in small words. Deal?"

Jessie nodded, offering ashy smile. "Deal."

As Zack made his way back to the counter, he couldn't help but glance back at Jessie. She'd already returned to her notebook, her tongue poking out slightly in concentration. It was, he had to admit, kind of adorable.

"Earth to Zack!" Reese's voice cut through his thoughts. He turned to find Beth's assistant manager grinning at him, a knowing look in her eyes. "You planning on making that coffee sometime today, or should I tell the doc to expect it next Christmas?"

Zack felt heat creep up his neck. "I was just... thinking about bean ratios."

"Uh-huh," Reese smirked. "And I'm the Queen of England. Spill, Harrington. What's with the googly eyes at our resident mad scientist?"

"There were no googly eyes," Zack protested, busying himself with the coffee grinder. "I'm just... scientifically curious."

Reese snorted. "Right. And I'm sure it has nothing to do with the way her hair catches the light, or how cute she looks when she's all flustered."

Zack nearly dropped the porta filter. "I... that's not... shouldn't you be at Sweet Dreams?"

"Day off," Reese shrugged. "Beth's too busy making heart eyes at her Belarusian beefcake to mind the store. Besides, someone's gotta keep an eye on you lovesick puppies."

Before Zack could formulate a response, the bell chimed again. Beth and Yuri walked in, hand in hand, looking disgustingly happy.

"Zack!" Beth called out; her smile radiant. "Just the man we wanted to see. Got a minute?"

Zack nodded, grateful for the distraction. "Sure, just let me deliver this coffee first."

He carefully carried the steaming cup to Jessie's table, setting it down next to a precariously balanced stack of textbooks. "One Brazilian single-origin, as requested. Careful, it's hot."

As Zack turned to head back to the counter, he noticed Beth, Yuri, and Reese entering the café. They waved him over, huddling near the pastry display with conspiratorial grins.

"Okay, what's going on?" Zack asked, crossing his arms. "You've all got that look."

"What look?" Beth asked, her eyes wide with faux innocence.

"The 'we're up to something and Zack's not going to like it' look," he replied dryly.

Yuri chuckled, slinging an arm around Beth's shoulders. "Can't put anything past you, my friend. We were just discussing the upcoming Valentine's Day festival."

Zack groaned. "Please tell me you're not roping me into another baking competition. My ego's still bruised from the last one."

"Not exactly," Beth said, her eyes twinkling. "We were thinking more along the lines of a collaboration. Sweet Dreams and The Daily Grind, joining forces to create the ultimate Valentine's Day treat."

Zack raised an eyebrow. "I'm listening."

"We were thinking of some sort of coffee-flavored dessert," Reese chimed in. "Something that combines Beth's baking skills with your coffee expertise."

Zack considered this fora moment. "That... actually sounds interesting. But why do I feel like there's more to this plan?"

The trio exchanged glances. "Well," Beth said slowly, "we thought it might be helpful to have a scientific perspective. You know, to really perfect the recipe. We were thinking of asking Jessie to join the project."

Zack's eyes narrowed. "Uh-huh. And I suppose it's just a coincidence that this collaboration would require me and Jessie to spend a lot of time together?"

"Purely professional, of course," Yuri added, his blue eyes twinkling with mischief.

Zack sighed, running a hand through his hair. "You guys are about as subtle as a sledgehammer, you know that?"

"Is that a yes?" Reese asked, grinning.

Zack glanced back at Jessie's table. She was now surrounded by a small crowd of curious onlookers, enthusiastically explaining something involving a lot of hand gestures and what looked like an impromptu diagram drawn on a napkin.

Despite himself, Zack felt a smile tugging at his lips. "Yeah, alright. I'm in. But!" he added quickly, seeing the triumphant looks on his friends' faces, "This is strictly a professional collaboration. Got it?"

"Of course," Beth nodded solemnly, though her eyes were dancing with barely suppressed glee. "Strictly professional. We'll go talk to Jessie now and see if she's interested."

As his friends moved towards Jessie's table, Zack found his gaze following them. He watched as they explained the project to Jessie, her eyes lighting up with excitement. She glanced over at him, offering a small wave and a smile that made his heart do a funny little flip.

Strictly professional. Right. Somehow, Zack had a feeling this Valentine's Day was going to beany thing but ordinary.

The rest of the afternoon passed in a blur of customers and coffee orders. Zack found himself stealing glances at Jessie's table whenever he had a free moment. She remained engrossed in her work, only occasionally surfacing to take a sip of her now-cold coffee or to answer a question from a curious patron.

As the crowd thinned out in the late afternoon lull, Zack decided to check on her. He approached the table, noting with amusement that she'd somehow managed to get a smudge of ink on her nose.

"Refill?" he asked, gesturing to her empty mug.

Jessie blinked up at him, as if surprised to find the café still existed outside her bubble of concentration. "Oh! Yes, please. That would be lovely."

As Zack turned to go, Jessie's hand shot out, grabbing his wrist. The sudden contact sent a jolt through him that had nothing to do with caffeine.

"Wait!" she said, her eyes bright with excitement. "I've had an idea. About the Valentine's Day project."

Zack raised an eyebrow. "Oh? I thought you were working on glaze viscosity or something."

Jessie waved a hand dismissively. "That was hours ago. Keep up, Harrington. No, I'm talking about the coffee-dessert hybrid. What if we approach it from a molecular gastronomy perspective?"

Despite his limited understanding of the term, Zack found himself intrigued. "Go on."

"Well," Jessie said, her words tumbling out in a rush of enthusiasm, "by manipulating the physical and chemical transformations of ingredients, we could potentially create entirely new textures and flavor combinations. Imagine a dessert that looks like a cappuccino but tastes like a tiramisu, or coffee caviar that bursts with flavor in your mouth!"

Zack couldn't help but smile at her excitement. "Sounds... intense. But interesting. You really think we could pull something like that off?"

Jessie's eyes met his, fierce and determined. "With your coffee expertise and my scientific know-how? Absolutely."

For a moment, they just looked at each other, a current of understanding passing between them. Then Zack cleared his throat, suddenly aware of how close they were standing.

"Well then, Dr. Brooke," he said, his voice a touch huskier than he'd intended, "I look forward to our collaboration."

As he walked back to the counter to get Jessie's refill, Zack couldn't shake the feeling that he'd just stepped onto a roller coaster he wasn't entirely prepared for. But as he glanced back to see Jessie already scribbling new ideas in her notebook, her face alight with enthusiasm, he realized something.

He couldn't wait for the ride to begin.

Milton Keynes UK
Ingram Content Group UK Ltd.
UKHW020258021124
450424UK00013B/1070